HUNG UP ON THE HACKER

A BEST FRIEND'S LITTLE SISTER, OOPS BABY,
SMALL TOWN, MILITARY ROMANCE

BAD BOY BAKERS
BOOK 4

KAIT NOLAN

TAKE THE LEAP PUBLISHING

A LETTER TO READERS

Dear Reader,

This book contains swearing and pre-marital sex between the lead couple, as those things are part of the realistic lives of characters of this generation, and of many of my readers.

If either of these things are not your cup of tea, please consider that you may not be the right audience for this book. There are scores of other books out there that are written with you in mind. In fact, I've got a list of some of my favorite authors who write on the sweeter side on my website at https://kaitnolan.com/on-the-sweeter-side/

If you choose to stick with me, I hope you enjoy!

Happy reading!

Kait

1

Tennessee: *The Volunteer State Welcomes You*

As the sign flashed by on I-81, Cash Grantham hit the voice controls on his steering wheel. "Call Hadley Steele."

The call connected, and the phone rang. And rang. And rang. Until her voicemail picked up. Again.

So, thirty-six hours hadn't been enough time for her to cool off. She could've been in the middle of work, but he knew her routine pretty well by now. After five phone calls, if she'd wanted to talk to him, she'd have picked up.

"Look, Hadley, I know you're pissed. I know you don't think this is necessary. But I swear to you, in the grand scheme of things, this is the right move. I'll come find you when I get back to town. Assuming your brother doesn't put me in the ground first."

It wasn't an unrealistic outcome. Cash had chosen to drive the seven-odd hours down from Baltimore to give himself time to consider his approach to this conversation, in hopes that it would remain civilized.

Holt Steele was one of his best friends. His brother in all

but blood. The man was the main reason Cash had survived growing up as the only child in an abusive, single-parent household. Holt had given him a safe place to land, when his mother couldn't be bothered to give a shit—which had been most of the time. She hadn't wanted him and had never made a secret of the fact that she hadn't been given a choice. She'd resented every second of his presence, every penny he'd cost. Cash didn't like thinking about where he'd have ended up without the Steele siblings. He knew well enough the horrors that had visited others in similar positions. Holt had always had his back. And Hadley... Hadley had given him a light in the darkness of a very grim childhood.

Cash didn't know exactly when things had changed. He'd always loved her, even when that bold, fiery spirit landed her in trouble that they'd had to bail her out from. Which had been often. But it had been the love of a brother. A friend. He wasn't sure precisely when he'd fallen for her. It was sometime after they'd reconnected, and he'd become aware that little Hadley Steele was all grown up and just as much of a ball buster as she'd always been. Damn, if he hadn't found that hot as hell.

He'd never intended to lay a hand on her. Best friend rules and all that. But she'd had other ideas, and he'd been powerless to resist her. He wasn't proud of how he'd justified it to himself, saying it was okay because they'd planned for their affair to be temporary. They'd both thought the heat between them would burn out and they'd move on, with Holt being none the wiser.

But Cash had gone and fallen in love with her.

He'd known it for a while and hadn't said a word. Hadley would probably bolt if he dropped the L-word. It was one thing for them to have fallen into something more serious. It was another thing to label it. She didn't trust in permanent relationships of a romantic variety. And why should she, after seeing her mom go through a parade of men, while more or less forgetting the fact she'd had two kids? So he'd put off dealing with the whole situation. But every day that passed, he'd felt more and more like shit that they were actively hiding their relationship from her brother. He'd finally hit his limit and put them on pause until he could talk to Holt.

Hadley hadn't taken it well. She was justifiably pissed at the idea that he was headed to Tennessee to get her brother's permission. She wasn't a possession. Wasn't Holt's to control. Cash understood that. But because of who Holt was to him, anything less than this was a betrayal. Really, the last six months of lies were already a massive breach of trust. Cash needed to make it right, and he could only hope like hell that the ring in his pocket would help them both forgive him.

But damn, he had no idea how he was going to bring up the topic with her incredibly overprotective brother—the former Army Ranger who knew a lot of ways to kill a man. He wouldn't be at all surprised if Holt wanted to kick his ass. It wasn't like Cash couldn't take on his buddy. He'd been Army Intelligence for a lot of years and was highly trained in his own way. Not to mention, they'd fought side-by-side for years growing up, so he knew how his friend moved. But if Holt needed to pound on him, Cash had no intention of stopping him. A bruising seemed like the least he owed his friend for the deception of the past six months. Then maybe Holt would actually give Cash the chance to explain that this wasn't a fleeting thing. He truly was in love with Hadley and wanted to make a life with her.

Would Holt think he was good enough for her? The stability Cash had created, the company he'd built using the skills he'd honed in the Army, and the money he'd accrued weren't the kind of things his friend gave a good damn about. They weren't the measure of a man. Not when you'd lived through hell together.

By the time he rolled into Eden's Ridge, Cash hadn't settled on any answers. It wasn't the first mission he'd worked with insufficient intel. He'd just have to play the whole damned thing by ear.

He hated playing things by ear.

Following the directions on his GPS, Cash drove to Bad Boy Bakers. It was a hell of a thing, knowing his friend had found a new purpose in opening a bakery with two other graduates from an experimental therapy program. But Holt was happy, and that was the only thing that mattered in the end.

Clad in dark green siding, the building itself sat partway up a hill, with the forested mountains stretching up behind it. Late autumn sun glinted off the tin roof. A few patrons sat on the wraparound porch, proving that winter was a long way from arriving here in East Tennessee. It was a little weird to see the place in person, since he was familiar with every angle of surveillance they had on the place, inside and out. But this was his first time actually visiting, despite repeated invitations from all three of the bakery's owners.

Cash climbed out of the car and headed for the door. A few more patrons occupied four-top tables inside. Courtesy of interior surveillance footage, he recognized the old geezers as regulars who liked to camp out and visit several times a week. They had the look of veterans about them, even without the trucker hat one of them sported with the Marine Corps coat of arms. Behind the counter, he spotted Jonah Ferguson and Brax Whitmore, both of Holt's business partners. They'd never met in person, but Cash was accustomed to being in situations where he knew more than everyone else in the room.

Jonah nodded a greeting. "Hey. Can we help you?"

Stuffing his hand into the pocket of his peacoat, Cash wrapped his fingers around the ring box. "Yeah. Holt here?"

The former SEAL didn't lose the friendly smile, but Cash saw the sharpening of his gaze and approved. "Who's asking?"

"Cash Grantham."

"Well, I'll be damned." Jonah skirted out from behind

the counter and came straight over, his hand extended. "It's good to finally meet you in person." The man's shake was firm.

"Likewise."

"We can't thank you enough for your help over the last year," Brax added, stepping up to offer his own hand.

Cash had turned his skills at espionage and hacking toward helping the three of them uncover who was behind a long string of harassment that had threatened the bakery and each of the women the bakers had fallen for. It had been a small thing in the scope of the sort of operations he ran most of the time. "Happy to help."

"Holt!" Jonah shouted. "Get out here."

The door that separated the kitchen from the front swung open, and Holt's familiar figure strode through. His smile spread wide at the sight of Cash. Unlike his partners, he didn't stop with just a handshake, pulling Cash in for a back-thumping hug.

"What the hell are you doing here, man?"

The box in Cash's pocket weighed on him like lead. For just a fleeting moment, he considered blurting it all out. But just in case Holt elected to deck him, he really didn't want that reputation for his friend's business. He'd sit on it until he could talk to Holt alone.

"Well, you said I should come down and visit. I thought I'd surprise you."

"About damned time." Holt glanced back at the kitchen. "Listen, I'm on deadline. I've got a cake I have to stay after closing to finish. How long are you in town?"

"Not sure. For the night, at least." He didn't know how long this was going to take. His team was taking care of things while he was gone, and he had his laptop to tackle anything that came up in the meantime.

"Do you have somewhere to stay?" Jonah asked. "The Misfit

Inn is the best place in town. Rachel's their new in-house baker." Pride in his fiancée shone in every word.

"I'll be sure to stop by and see if I can get a room."

"Fantastic. And you'll come to dinner tonight," Holt insisted.

"Is that going to be okay with Cayla? Do you really want to surprise your wife with a dinner guest?"

Holt waved his concern away. "It'll be fine."

God, Cash hoped so. He figured if he waited until they got to the house, around Holt's wife and daughter, maybe he'd be less inclined to commit violence. If everything went smoothly, he could be back on the road tomorrow to go fix things with his woman.

"All right then. Dinner it is."

HADLEY STEELE HATED BEING WRONG. She hated admitting it even more. But she'd been taught by her mule-headed big brother to own up to her mistakes. If she'd chosen to do that in her own way, on her own terms, rather than accepting any of Cash's calls, well, all three of them knew she was the most stubborn of their trio. So she'd gotten on the road at an entirely unreasonable hour this morning, to drive down to Tennessee and talk to Holt herself.

If he lost his shit over her involvement with his best friend, he wouldn't hit her. She didn't have the same confidence about his restraint when it came to Cash. What *was* it about brothers and their friends when it came to little sisters? That protectiveness made sense when she'd been young, but she was a grown-ass woman who made her own decisions about who she let into her bed. She had plenty of choice arguments to make about the subject, and she was prepared to deliver them at top volume if necessary. She just hoped she got to him before Cash did.

Obstinate, honorable, sexy man.

Was it any wonder she was totally gone over him?

Not wanting to confront Holt at work, she'd timed her arrival, hoping to catch him at home. She knew that most days he picked up his adopted daughter Maddie from school when he finished up at the bakery. With luck, they'd be smack dab in the middle of snack time and homework. Was she hoping her niece would be an inadvertent buffer? Hell yes. Hadley knew how to work her brother, and she wasn't above taking every potential advantage she could to minimize the inevitable explosion.

Pulling up to the curb several houses down from the little bungalow her brother called home, she took a moment to wipe damp palms on her jeans. It would be fine. Holt would probably be upset to start, for all the reasons Cash had outlined yesterday morning. He *was* likely to see their subterfuge as a betrayal. She didn't think her reasons for not telling him were bad ones, but Cash had a point about not wanting to sneak around for the long haul. Which implied he also believed there would be a long haul. She wanted that more than she could admit, so no matter what Holt thought about it, she'd make him see reason. She absolutely would not allow him to end his friendship with Cash over this. Not when she knew how much that relationship meant to Cash.

Hadley climbed out of her car, pausing for a moment to strike a power pose, hands on hips, shoulders thrown back. She could do this. She was a badass. With a deep breath, she strode down the street and up the walk, past the bright-faced pansies in the neat little beds that provided a pop of color in the late autumn landscape, and on up to the cheerful blue front door. Her knock was greeted by a volley of frenetic barking from Banana Bread, the family mutt. Moments later, the door was yanked open, and a pint-sized blonde dervish shrieked, "Aunt Hadley!"

Maddie leapt, wrapping her little arms and legs around Hadley with all the excited joy a six-year-old could muster.

Delighted, Hadley hugged her back, inhaling the scents of bubble gum and... was that popcorn? "Hey, Pipsqueak."

Maddie's mother, Cayla, appeared in the doorway, her smile spreading wide. "Hadley! What are you doing here?" Any possible censure in the question was erased by the warm side hug she wrapped around Hadley's shoulders.

"Well, I did promise I'd come back. I thought I'd pop down for a surprise visit."

"That's wonderful. Holt will be so happy to see you."

Hadley shifted Maddie to one hip. "Is he home?"

"Not just yet. He's staying late to work on a cake, but he'll be home by dinner."

So she'd be getting a little reprieve. That was fine. It would give her the opportunity to get the lay of the land before she had to face him.

Cayla glanced back at the street and frowned. "Where's your car?"

"Down the street. The better to surprise him."

"Fair enough. Come in! Come in!"

"Come play with me!" Maddie demanded.

"Homework first," her mother ordered. "You only have one more worksheet left."

As her niece's bottom lip began to roll out, Hadley rushed to intervene. "Finish your homework, and I'll give you a marker tattoo before dinner. Does that work for you?"

"Yeah!" When she squirmed, Hadley let her down, and she went racing off to the kitchen.

Cayla shook her head, a fond smile curving her lips. "Oh, to have that level of energy."

"No kidding." After the seven-hour drive, Hadley was dragging. She'd slept like shit last night, not in Cash's bed. It annoyed her she'd gotten so comfortable there. She'd more or less moved in over the past couple of months, and now the tidy little studio apartment above her shop just wasn't the same.

"Want coffee?"

"That would be awesome."

Hadley trailed her sister-in-law into the kitchen and slid onto one of the barstools at the counter. "So, how is everybody?"

Cayla began puttering around, putting on a pot. "Busy as all get out, but good. I'm up to my eyeballs planning a bunch of holiday weddings. The guys are doing really well. They're looking at expanding into some mail-order business after the first of the year."

Hadley listened as she talked and concluded that Holt didn't know yet and had said nothing to his wife. As an event planner, Cayla was too much a romantic not to comment on it if he had. Instead, she prattled on about married and domestic things, clearly content. It was so... normal. Or at least what Hadley imagined was normal. Her brother deserved as much of that as he could get.

A few minutes later, Cayla settled on the next stool, sliding over a mug. "Now, tell me everything about what's going on with you."

Well, that was a tall order.

Hadley opened her mouth, intent on bringing Cayla into her confidence and asking for some assistance in managing her brother.

"Done!" Maddie threw up her hands, as if completing math worksheets was a competitive sport. "Marker tattoos!"

Chickening out, Hadley swallowed the words. "Go get your markers, then."

Maddie scampered out of the room, the golden-furred BB on her heels.

"I should've asked first. Are you okay if I draw all over her?"

Cayla grinned. "As long as you're not using permanent ink."

"I can work with that. You're such a good mom. Maddie's lucky to have you." Certainly, Hadley's own mother hadn't won any awards for her parenting skills. She'd been an unavoidable cautionary tale.

"She's a great kid."

Feeling far too exposed under Cayla's empathetic gaze, Hadley cleared her throat and deflected. "So, are you and Holt planning on giving me a new niece or nephew anytime soon?"

Her sister-in-law's cheeks heated, her eyes darting to the doorway her daughter had just exited. "We're working on it."

It was Hadley's turn to grin. Holt was happy and settled here. Family life suited him down to the ground, which had been a surprise to them both. But having the choice, rather than being forced into it, as he had at far too young an age when he'd taken on the job of raising her, made all the difference. Hadley loved the little family he'd stumbled into. Loved that they were hers now, too, because he'd made that choice. Family was everything to them both. The one they'd been born into hadn't been worth a damn, so they'd made their own little unit.

Cash had been a part of that unit for so long, her memories of him went back almost as far as those of her brother. He'd been another protector, another playmate, another friend. Of course, once she'd hit adolescence, she'd had the world's biggest crush on him. That was part and parcel of growing up. But she'd never imagined *doing* anything about it. Not until he'd strode into her shop earlier this year and asked her to design a half-sleeve tattoo to cover that magnificent shoulder and biceps. She'd all but drowned in lust the moment she'd laid eyes on him again. And—wonder of wonders—she'd seen the same reflected in his dark brown eyes.

They were explosive together. She'd known they would be. But she'd thought the heat would burn itself out once their curiosity was satisfied, which was how she'd convinced him *not* to talk to Holt straight out of the gate. She hadn't meant for this to happen. Things had gotten out of hand and turned serious a lot faster than—well, she hadn't expected them to turn serious at all. Neither of them had been looking for serious, and they'd both been very careful not to talk about what came next.

Until yesterday, when suddenly Cash had hit his limit and declared them on a "pause" until her brother could be informed. As if their intimate relationship was any of his business.

Not that they'd clarified a damned thing about that relationship, beyond the fact that they didn't intend to break things off. Never mind that she'd stormed out of Cash's apartment in a snit. He knew she'd be back. So did she. Which meant she had to suck it up to do the hard thing. Damn it.

Maddie came running back in, a pack of markers in her hand.

Carrying her coffee to the table, Hadley sat and helped the child roll up her sleeve. "What would you like, kiddo?"

"A mermaid!"

Hadley nodded soberly. "A classic for a reason." After checking to make sure the markers were washable, she took Maddie's hand and turned it this way and that, taking in the shape of her canvas and letting her brain paint the image there. Then she put marker to skin and began bringing the image to life.

Dimly, she was aware of Cayla moving around the kitchen, probably pulling out the beginnings of dinner. Maddie kept up a steady stream of chatter that Hadley answered with half an ear. Most of her focus was on the drawing, coaxing the colors into focus. Markers wouldn't allow her to achieve the detail of the true picture in her mind, but she figured Maddie would be happy with the end result. The process relaxed her, getting her out of her head and away from the spinning anxiety of what was to come.

At least until Maddie yanked her hand free, shouting, "Daddy!" She leapt up, making a beeline for the garage door, where Holt scooped her up.

"Hey, Bumblebee."

Maddie looped her arms around his neck. "Look who came to visit!"

"That's what I was going to say." Eyes on Hadley, he moved out of the doorway.

And there, standing behind him, was Cash.

Well, shit.

2

The moment Cash spotted Hadley's familiar, purple-streaked espresso brown hair, everything inside him lifted and brightened with relief. He itched to cross the room, haul her into his arms and erase the distance he'd put between them. Somewhere, deep down, a part of him had watched her walk away yesterday and worried she wouldn't come back. People had done that often enough in his life.

But not Hadley. Never Hadley.

She was bold and brash and unapologetic in how she lived. Cash recognized that if she was really through with him, there'd have been a declarative announcement about it at earsplitting decibel, probably with considerable profanity and significant possibility of projectiles of convenience.

Instead, she was here.

Oh shit. She was *here*.

Did this mean she'd come around to his way of thinking? Recognizing that they had to clear the air with Holt if they were going to continue? Or had she driven all this way with some intention of stopping him?

There was no way to ask her, and her very presence threw a big ass monkey wrench into his plans.

"—daughter, Maddie. And my wife, Cayla."

Cash dragged his focus over to the pair of pretty blondes, the one in Holt's arms, a miniature of the woman beaming in his direction.

He plastered on a smile to hide the inner turmoil. "Nice to meet you both, finally." And he meant it. These two might have become Holt's family through a marriage of convenience meant to protect Cayla and her daughter from the ex-husband that had been released from prison back in the spring, but they were truly his now. They'd given his friend a place to land, and Cash would be forever grateful for that. Holt deserved that kind of happy ending after all the shit he'd been through in his life and his military service.

And so did he. Cash couldn't stop his gaze from shifting back to Hadley. He wanted to be her safe place to land. Wanted her to be his. It took all his training to bury that emotion down deep instead of reaching out to touch her, claim her, anything to reassure himself that she was still his.

"Didn't know you were coming down."

Her gray eyes sparked with mischief rather than temper, and that was enough to tell him she wasn't here to fight. "It was spur of the moment. You know me."

He certainly did. Far better than her brother could possibly be aware.

"Too bad you didn't communicate," Cayla said. "Y'all could've carpooled down together."

Hadley scoffed. "And let Mr. High and Mighty control the stereo? No, thank you. Seven hours of the same three bands is not for me."

"And seven hours of eighties throwbacks is better?" Cash shot back, relieved to fall into the familiar dynamic.

She gave an imperious lift of her chin. "It was the best

music decade. Full of power ballads and full-bodied rock and roll."

"You keep telling yourself that, sweetheart."

Holt rolled his eyes and set Maddie down. "They've been having this argument for fifteen years."

"Two words." Cash pointed to Hadley. "Tone. Deaf."

She sniffed. "You just can't appreciate my vocal stylings."

"Is that what you're calling your caterwauling now?" Holt asked.

Maddie tugged at his pant leg. "Daddy, what's caterwilling?"

Daddy. Damn. Holt really had landed himself a real live nuclear family. It wasn't something he'd had growing up. Wasn't something either of them had had. It meant something to Cash to see it was possible. That it could really work. It made him feel like this thing he wanted wasn't so insane or out of reach as it had felt on the drive down.

"Caterwauling," Holt corrected. "You ever hear a couple of cats fighting?"

Maddie shook her head. "Uh-uh."

"Well, it's not a pretty sound. That's what your Aunt Hadley sounds like when she sings."

The subject of their teasing stuck her tongue out.

The kid's eyes got big as saucers. "You mean... she can't sing good like you can?"

"Can't carry a tune in a bucket," Cash informed her. "Your dad got all the musical talent in the family."

"Not that it ever stopped Had from trying."

Hadley crossed her arms with a huff. "What I lack in skill, I make up for with enthusiasm."

Cayla snickered and shot a significant look at her daughter. "Sounds like someone else I know."

"Maybe my genes will win out with the next one." Holt grinned and tugged his wife in for a kiss.

"The next one?" Cash blinked and glanced at Cayla. "Are you—?"

She just smiled. "Not yet. But that's the plan."

"Wow. Congrats. Good luck with that."

Another kid. On purpose. Cash couldn't quite wrap his brain around it. He'd never thought about children. He wasn't a guy who'd thought much about the future. Not beyond the end of the week. The month. The mission. For so much of his life, there'd been no guarantee that he'd have a future. But being with Hadley had made him dream about it.

He could see her in his future. Wanted her as his wife. But he hadn't thought beyond that to what their life together would look like. Obviously, that wasn't something he could decide on his own. He had to actually have a conversation with her. And there were all those pertinent details, like telling her he loved her and asking her to marry him, and so on and so forth. Talking about the future that they'd been very careful to tiptoe around all these months as she'd slowly, inexorably become entwined in his life.

He wondered how she'd feel about the idea of family. Of kids. Was she as leery of all that as he was? With what they'd both come from, he wouldn't be surprised if she also felt a bit at war with herself over the subject. Would they be doomed to repeat the mistakes of their parents? God knew they'd had terrible examples. Or would they make better parents because they knew the things not to do?

It hardly mattered. The entire subject was very much getting ahead of things. They simply weren't there yet, and he needed to slow his roll. But standing in this cozy kitchen, with his brother of the heart and his family, for the first time, Cash thought he wanted to look into all of it.

～

HADLEY GLANCED up and down the hall of The Misfit Inn. Cash's room was on the third floor—a fact she knew courtesy of the innkeeper's excessively romantic, matchmaking teenage daughter, whom she'd met on a prior visit.

Thank you, Ari.

So long as she was quick, nobody would be around to see. Tugging a couple of bobby pins from her hair, she bent to the lock, sliding them in and carefully working the tumblers. Five seconds later, she slipped inside, quietly closing the door. Cash wouldn't be far behind. She had maybe a five- or ten-minute lead on him leaving her brother's house.

Slipping the pins into her pocket, she prowled the room. The queen-size bed butted up against the one flat wall. The rest of the room was octagonal, in the turret of the old Victorian that had been converted to a B and B. Lace curtains hung at the many windows looking out over what she knew would be a gorgeous view of the Appalachians once the sun rose. For now, the dark pressed in, lending a sense of intimacy to the space. It was a romantic room. One of the few in the inn with an en-suite bath. A clawfoot tub was tucked inside, next to a pedestal sink. Under other circumstances, she'd have run a bath and been waiting for Cash when he got back. But at the moment, they needed to clear the air. She had apologies to make.

Exhausted from keeping up the just-friends act all through dinner, Hadley dropped onto his bed to wait, snuggling into the soft down comforter and cozy pillows.

What felt like seconds later, a rough male voice rasped in her ear. "Who's this sleeping in my bed like Goldilocks?"

She blinked her eyes open, realizing she'd fallen asleep.

Cash braced himself over her, his eyes full of amusement and heat. "Did you steal a key?"

Her lips twitched. "Who needs a key? I was taught to pick locks by one of the best."

As that had been him, he was hardly in a position to argue.

He huffed a laugh.

Before he could pull back, she reached up to stroke a hand along the dark scruff of his cheek. "I'm sorry for walking out yesterday. It seemed a better alternative than raging at you."

"I could've handled it better. Springing that on you right after you woke up, before you'd even had coffee, was not my brightest decision."

To say Hadley wasn't a morning person was a vast under-statement. Her business stayed open late, so she started late, and she liked it that way.

"Notes for the future," she quipped.

His gaze turned serious. "You want there to be one?"

Her heart began to pound out a drum solo. How could she say an unequivocal yes? No matter how much she wanted it, the idea of admitting it out loud absolutely terrified her. So she deflected. "I don't want there *not* to be one. And I get where you're coming from. Why we have to tell Holt. That's why I came down. I thought if I was here, the explosion wouldn't be quite as big. Because I really don't expect him to take this well. That was part of why I didn't want to tell him in the first place."

"It's why I let you talk me out of it. But that was the coward's way, and now we'll have to deal with the consequences."

"Deal with them over here." She tugged him down onto the bed, loving the brief feel of his weight covering her before he rolled over, pulling her into the shelter of his body. As it was exactly what she'd wanted, she snuggled in with a sigh. "That's better. Missed you last night."

His lips brushed her temple. "Missed you, too."

They lay like that for long moments, and she wondered that just being quiet with him could feel this comforting. He'd always protected her, but this was different. In his arms, she found safety and unreserved acceptance. That was one of the greatest gifts he'd ever given her.

She was, as people were prone to say, "a lot." She was loud, opinionated, determined, and she had absolutely no compunction about telling anyone exactly what she thought. Pussyfooting around was inefficient. Why not get straight to the point? More than one adult had told her to "tone it down" over the years. That just made Hadley dig in her heels to be even more unabashedly herself. The wild hair colors, the tattoos that had begun as defiance and become her art, her livelihood. If people judged her for all that—and they definitely did—well, that was a *them* problem.

But she was deathly afraid that her brother would judge her for this relationship with Cash. And she had no intention of letting him take all the blame. It had been her idea to change things. She who'd shocked the hell out of him one night, by kissing him when he'd walked her up to her apartment door, long after closing. She who'd dragged him inside.

Not that she wanted to give Holt all the details, but she'd do what needed doing to deflect his anger.

Cash threaded his fingers into her hair, massaging at the tension at the base of her skull. "So, let's make a plan. Go through the whole thing. What are you afraid of in all this?"

"That he'll be pissed. That he'll take that out on you. I don't want you to lose him. If I'd thought for a moment you would, I'd never have kissed you." She paused, considering. Her impulse control wasn't good enough to have stopped her from satisfying that lifelong curiosity. "Or at least I wouldn't have taken it further than that."

"We'd have both missed out if you hadn't."

It pleased her to hear it. Trailing her fingers along his muscled forearm, she pressed a kiss against his throat. "I don't want to lose him either."

"You're never going to lose Holt. There's nothing on earth you could do to make him walk away from you."

"Maybe not, but I could disappoint him, and that's just as bad. He's my only family, Cash."

"How could you possibly disappoint him?"

There were things in her past she'd gone out of her way to avoid him ever finding out. Things she'd never, ever tell him. Things she didn't intend to tell Cash, either. The two of them were cut from the same cloth. What was past was best left in the past.

"There are ways." Not wanting to continue with that line of questioning, she tipped her head back. "What about you? What are you most concerned about?"

He sighed, his chest rising and falling against hers. "I'm pretty worried he'll be pissed as hell and won't be able to forgive me for touching you. I'm afraid of losing my friend. My brother. We should have told him at the start."

Hadley hit him with some hefty side eye. "Really? You think that would have gone better? If you'd asked his permission or blessing to see me as something other than a sister or friend, do you think he'd really have given it? Do you think my brother was ever going to give any guy permission to jump into my bed?"

"Well, I don't have a death wish. I wasn't going to ask it like that. And that's not what this is."

"Now it's not," she conceded. "But that's how it started. That's all we expected in the beginning. And we were both okay with that."

The hand on her nape went still. "Is that all you want still?"

Hadley stayed silent for a long time. She could deflect again. It was probably what he expected. But it was the second time he'd asked about where she saw the relationship going, and here in his bed, in this cozy mountain inn, she felt as if she owed him the truth.

"No. No, that's not all I want."

She waited for him to press her.

Instead, he resumed massaging her neck. "Okay, then. So how do we handle this? A united front? One-on-one?"

"I don't know. I feel like there has to be an answer that's going to mitigate the damage. I'm inclined to think it's better coming from me. Either me on my own or the two of us together. I don't think you should talk to him by yourself. Because I really don't know what he's gonna do. I mean, for all intents and purposes, he's become this laid-back family guy, which is weird as hell and wonderful to see. But I don't have a lot of confidence that he'll stay that way when it comes to me. You know how protective he's always been."

"Yeah, I do. I'm the same way." Cash lapsed into silence, and she could all but hear the gears in his big brain turning. Considering angles, running scenarios in his head. She wouldn't put it past him to set up some kind of computer program to assess the odds.

"I'm afraid he won't think I'm good enough for you."

Hadley exploded up. "What?" She didn't know which part to be more upset with. "How dare you think so little of yourself? You're one of the best men I know. One of the best men Holt knows. That's been true since we were kids. Look what you've made of yourself. Especially considering where you started."

Unperturbed, Cash only shrugged. "You and I both know those aren't the things Holt cares about."

"Maybe not." She leaned down, framing his face in both hands and pressing her brow to his. "You are a good man, Cash. I wouldn't be with you if you weren't. At the end of the day, that's the only thing that matters. And if Holt doesn't see that, then he's not the friend or brother either of us believes him to be."

Cash tightened his arms, pulling her flush against him. "I don't think we're going to come up with a clear plan tonight. You look wiped."

"I am. Apparently, fighting takes a lot out of me."

"Then we should get some sleep. Actual sleep," he added.

Hadley winced. Evidently, he was sticking to this whole "pause" on the intimate side of their relationship until this was sorted. "Are you going to make me go back to my room?"

"Only to get your stuff."

"Thank God."

3

C ash woke long before dawn, his mind and arms full
of Hadley. He ought to have used the time to plan the
best approach to talking to Holt. Instead, he lay in
the dark, breathing in her sleep-warmed scent, lingering in the
feeling of absolute rightness, having her sprawled beside him.
Even the fact that she took up more than her half of the queen-
sized bed made him smile. She never questioned her right to be
anywhere, ever. That unapologetic nature was something he'd
always loved about her. So much of his own life had been spent
fighting for his place.

Would Holt make him fight for his place with her? And if it
came down to it and Cash was forced to choose, which way
would he go? The idea of losing either of them cut him deep.
But it wasn't a choice. Not really. He loved Holt as a brother, but
he was in love with Hadley. Of course, all that presupposed she
chose him if given the same ultimatum. Some men might make
that call for her, simply walking away in some self-sacrificial
gesture. Even if he hadn't known better—and he did—he was
too selfish for that. If there was a chance in hell Hadley would

choose him, he was taking it. And he'd spend the rest of their lives making sure she didn't regret it.

As daylight crept across the foot of the bed, he carefully eased away from her. She merely rolled into the warm spot he vacated, curling up like a cat. Grinning to himself, he tugged on jeans and a sweater, running his hands through his hair. They were on no schedule today, with nowhere to be. He'd leave her sleeping. Slipping out of the room, he silently shut the door behind him.

A sound had him whipping toward the stairwell.

Ari Bohannon, the innkeepers' daughter, stood by the window, one dark brow arched and a knowing smirk on her face.

Putting on his best bland nothing-to-see-here face, Cash strode toward the girl, nodding a greeting. Ari nodded back, barely swallowing a grin, before trotting down the stairs ahead of him.

Damn it. He should have made Hadley go to her own room last night. But he'd missed her. Missed having her in his bed beside him, knowing she was close enough to take care of. Not that she'd appreciate the sentiment. She valued her independence and the fact that she could take care of herself. With her history, she'd never want to be a burden on anyone. But that wasn't what this was. He just wanted to look out for her. She wasn't a morning person to begin with, and she'd been extra tired lately. It wasn't exactly a surprise. They'd essentially traded orgasms for good nights' sleep for months. But this seemed like more than that, and he was low-key worried about it. Maybe she needed more iron. She was prone to living off pasta and not much else when she got busy at work. When was the last time she'd had a physical?

As it was midweek and still early, no one else was in the dining room. Cash helped himself to the coffee laid out on a sideboard before settling at one of the tables by the window, his back to the corner. Some habits couldn't be easily broken.

A tall, willowy blonde came in. "Good morning! You must be Cash. I've heard... well, honestly, not an enormous amount about you."

Recognizing Jonah's fiancée from the surveillance he'd done, he answered her smile. "That's a calculated move. I'm a man of mystery. You must be Rachel. Congrats on the engagement."

She beamed, happiness practically radiating out of every pore. "Thanks! Jonah and I are gearing up for a winter wedding to avoid the busy season at the bakery."

Cash wondered what constituted the busy season for a bakery. "Seems sensible."

"What are you in the mood for this morning?" She nodded toward a narrow folio tucked in the condiments. "Those are our regular options. But since it's just you, I can whip up something off-menu, if you like. Eggs of some kind, if you're not looking for something baked. If you're still here by the weekend, we'll have the full Southern available."

"What exactly is that?"

"Biscuits and gravy, bacon or sausage, eggs, and grits."

Knowing she was from upstate New York, Cash lifted a brow. "Can you actually cook a full Southern?"

Rachel dimpled. "I promise I've been taught by true Southerners how to make proper grits. And I've had biscuits in the bag for years."

"Good to know. Could I get an omelet?"

"Sure thing. What would you like in it?"

"Meat, veggies, and cheese. I'm not fussy about what kind. Surprise me."

"You've got it." At the door, she turned back. "Does Holt know?"

"Does Holt know what?"

"About you and Hadley."

Cash froze, the mug of coffee halfway to his mouth.

Shit. Shit. Shit.

Evidently, Ari had shared what she saw in the kitchen.

"I'm not letting the cat out of the bag. I'm just confirming the status and whether I need to keep my mouth shut. Even from Jonah."

Keeping that same bland expression in place, he settled back in his chair, as if he wasn't secretly freaking out. "No, he doesn't know. That's why we're here."

Rachel nodded. "Understood."

Only after she'd disappeared back to the kitchen did he release the breath caught in his chest. He didn't like having any more people in the circle of knowledge before he had a chance to talk to his friend. That meant more people who could inadvertently spill the beans. They really needed to get on this.

He was halfway through his cup of coffee when Hadley stumbled into the dining room, looking only half-conscious. Dropping down on the opposite side of the table, she folded her arms and put her head down with a bit of a whimper.

"Are you okay?" Dumb question. Clearly, she wasn't.

"I don't feel great. I was in a hurry to get down yesterday, and my lunch was a gas station hotdog. I'm thinking that was a grave mistake."

Rachel swung through the door on the tail end of this explanation. "Oh, you poor thing. Can I get you some ginger ale? Some peppermint tea? Maybe a little oatmeal to settle your stomach?"

Hadley lifted her head, focusing on the other woman with heavy eyes. "That would be great. All the above, if possible."

"I'll be back in just a minute."

Cash studied her closer, noting the puffiness beneath her eyes and the slightly wan cheeks. "Maybe you should go back to bed."

That she didn't snark back with something sexy proved she wasn't herself.

"I'm sure I'll feel better with food. Whatever this is just needs to work its way out of my system."

Rachel returned with a tall glass of iced ginger ale and a steaming mug with the string of a tea bag hanging down the side.

"You are a goddess." Hadley pounced on the ginger ale, gulping it down.

"I'll have that oatmeal right out. Do you want it plain? With fruit? Maple brown sugar?"

"She likes cinnamon and apples." The words were out before Cash could think better of them.

Hadley, now with her nose practically buried in the tea mug, offered a thumbs up.

"On it."

When they were alone again, she curled her hands around the mug, studying him over the rim. "You know how I like my oatmeal."

He shrugged. "You always stole the apple cinnamon from the multi-packs of instant when we were kids."

Her lips curved. "It was your fault. You got me started on it. Before then, it was all Holt's maple brown sugar. Finding out there were other flavors kind of blew my mind."

Eating flavored oatmeal at all had been a luxury. They'd all grown up in such poverty, it was a wonder they had any fond memories at all. But she was at the center of so many of his. A huge part of his mission in life back then had been to make her smile. To distract her from her mom's latest bender or the fighting with her latest beau. And part of it had been diverting her with food, giving her the apple cinnamon oatmeal because she loved it, even though it was his favorite, too.

Rachel returned once more, a bowl and plate in her hands.

She slid the oatmeal in front of Hadley and set a fluffy, golden omelet in front of him.

Cash couldn't resist a sniff. "This smells amazing. Thank you."

"Enjoy! And let me know if you need anything else."

She disappeared, and Hadley took a testing bite, letting out a low moan that had Cash's body stirring. "This is amazing. I wonder if I can sweet talk them out of the recipe."

Jonah owed him a favor. If Rachel didn't outright share it, he'd call it in.

Cash dug into his omelet, enjoying the blend of smoked ham, cheddar, onions, and peppers. "I was reading on the menu that most of the food is provided by Maxwell Organics, here in Eden's Ridge."

"Oh yeah. Logan Maxwell is married to Athena Reynolds. She's one of the quartet of sisters who opened this place. Award-winning chef. Used to have some fancy restaurant in Chicago before coming back here. Now she's got an online cooking show and a cookbook."

Impressed with the summary, he arched a brow. "Where'd you get all that?"

Hadley spooned up more oatmeal. "Ari. She told me all about it on my previous stay."

"So, she's a talker." He'd been afraid of that.

"A good-natured one. Why?"

"She knows where you spent the night last night. Hence, so does Rachel. Who offered assurances she'd keep her mouth shut."

"It'll be fine." Unperturbed, Hadley kept eating her oatmeal.

The phone she'd set on the edge of the table vibrated with a text. She nodded toward it. "You wanna check that?"

Cash tipped the screen up to read the message. "It's Cayla. There's apparently gonna be a big group dinner with everybody tonight at six. Cookout with the whole bakery crew and their significant others."

"Tell her we'll be there."

He went brows up. "You want me to answer for both of us? That's a hell of a couply thing to do."

His own phone vibrated from his pocket.

"That's probably yours."

He checked the readout, confirming her assumption. "Your brother. Same invite."

Swiping open both phones, he sent back individual texts in the affirmative. No reason to borrow trouble yet. Setting them aside, he dug back into the rest of his omelet.

"How are you feeling?" Her color was better.

Hadley sat back in her chair, the bowl in front of her empty. "More like a human. Maybe my blood sugar tanked or something. Food helped."

"Good. Now, since it's the middle of everybody's work week, and we're free until dinner, what do you want to do today?"

AFTER CONSIDERABLE DISCUSSION, Hadley and Cash had opted to show up for dinner separately. Neither of them felt that breaking the news of their involvement to Holt in front of a mass gathering was wise, even if at least one of the people attending was aware of it. He wouldn't appreciate being blindsided. They'd have to bide their time for another day. She was glad she'd cleared her appointments for the rest of the week. If this went badly, she'd need some time to process before picking up her tattoo gun again.

Courtesy of a nap that ran longer than she'd intended, Hadley was the last to arrive. She'd sent Cash on ahead while she showered and made herself presentable. Pulling in the drive beside his fully restored vintage black Mustang, she checked her reflection in the visor mirror. A couple of hours at the Misfit Spa, along with her nap and judicious application of makeup, had erased the last signs of whatever stomach thing had plagued her this morning. Satisfied, she made her way to the front door, knocking once before figuring she was family and pushing it open.

She was not prepared for the chaos waiting inside. Music and laughter filled the space, punctuated by joyful barking from multiple dogs. As she shut the door, a behemoth pit bull, with the biggest head she'd ever seen, came charging toward her, tongue lolling.

"Uh." Hadley backed up to the door.

"Leno!" A sharp female voice arrested the dog's forward momentum.

Leno's butt dropped, so that he skidded forward on the hardwood floors, bumping into Hadley's knees with that massive head. He woofed and nudged again, *smiling* at her. She'd never seen a dog smile before.

A gorgeous Latina woman with a toddler on her hip emerged from the kitchen. "Sorry. He thinks all new people live to adore him."

"Oh." Reassured she wasn't about to be eaten, Hadley dropped her hand to the dog's head, scratching between his ears.

Leno's doggy grin spread wider in ecstasy, one foot beginning to thump.

"There now. You're friends for life. C'mon, pal. Let's go outside with the others. B.B., Otis! Out! Outside." At her order, Banana Bread and a big-footed puppy appeared from nowhere and stampeded toward the door to the backyard.

Rachel opened it, calling, "Incoming!"

Cayla stepped out of the kitchen. "Good call. Oh, you're here!" She hurried over to wrap Hadley in a hug. "Can I take your coat?"

"Sure." Hadley slid off the bold red, faux fur jacket Cash swore looked like she'd murdered a Muppet. "What can I do to help?"

"Not a thing. The guys are all outside manning the grill. I think you've met Rachel already. And this is Mia, Brax's wife."

Mia lifted her chin in acknowledgement and angled the little boy her way. "And this is Duncan, our foster son. Can you say hi?"

Without a word, Duncan hid his face against her neck.

"We're a little overwhelmed." Tightening her arms around the child, Mia pressed a kiss to his tousled brown hair.

The gesture made Hadley's throat tighten. Some women were just maternal. She hadn't expected that of Brax's contractor wife, but it just went to show that those instincts were in there for a lot of women. Her mom definitely hadn't been one of them, and Hadley was pretty sure she didn't have the gene either. That was fine. She was rocking favorite aunt territory.

Shaking off the feeling, she offered them a smile. "Totally understandable."

"His sister, Dakota, is around here somewhere. Probably near Brax. Those two are thick as thieves."

"And no wonder, given all the upheaval they've had," Cayla said.

Mia's expression sobered. "Never again. We've still got a few months before the adoption can be finalized, but our social worker is hopeful, and so are we."

Hadley knew from her brother that Mia and her husband had been foster kids themselves, so it didn't surprise her they'd opted to go that route for their family. What would her life have been like if Holt hadn't broken his back to make sure she was taken care of so that Social Services didn't come sniffing around? She didn't know what these kids had come from, but she could take a guess.

"They'll definitely be better off with you two as parents."

Mia smiled, snuggling her son. "We think so."

"We're not too far out from dinner," Rachel put in. "What's your pleasure to drink? Are you feeling better?"

"Much, thanks. Food and a nap and some pampering did the trick. Iced tea is fine."

"Oh, were you sick?" Cayla asked.

"Just a little stomach thing this morning. No big deal."

The back door opened again, and Holt strode inside. "Oh hey, Squirt."

"Jerkface."

Her brother grinned before turning to his wife. "Hey babe, where's the marinade? I need to baste the chicken again."

Cayla handed over a jar and basting brush, accepting a lingering kiss. Yep, totally nutso for each other. That new niece or nephew would be coming along any time now.

Through the still open door, Hadley got a whiff of whatever was cooking and felt her stomach pitch. The hard, sharp certainty that she was about to vomit had her making excuses. "I'm just gonna go use the restroom before dinner."

The door to the hall bathroom was closed and locked.

Crap. Bile rose in her throat. She did not want to throw up in front of everyone.

"Oh, one of the kids is in there. Go on back to our room," Cayla called.

Shooting her a thumbs up, Hadley made her way to the master bedroom, just barely managing not to run. As soon as she shut the door, she bolted for the bathroom, shutting that door, too, before stumbling toward the toilet and dropping to her knees to retch. Very little came up, but her stomach continued to cramp. She curled over the bowl for a couple minutes until the wave passed. Cautiously optimistic it was over, she wiped her mouth with a wad of tissue and sank back against the wall, trying to catch her breath.

What the hell was going on? Food poisoning shouldn't last this long. And she'd felt absolutely fine after she'd eaten this morning. Why did this nausea keep coming back? Some kind of blood sugar issue? A stomach bug?

Her gaze fell to the open box of pregnancy tests on the back of the toilet and the bottom dropped out of her world.

No. Oh no. It can't be that.

Her mind scrambled to do the math. What the hell day was it? She counted back, then forward again. *Shit. Shit!* She should've started more than a week ago. Work had been insane, and she'd been focused on Cash, then on being pissed at Cash.

It might be nothing. It couldn't be this. They'd been careful, always using birth control. She was on the pill, and they always used condoms. Well, except for once or twice in the shower. They were responsible, damn it. She'd have insisted on it, even if he hadn't. So it couldn't be *that.*

But what if it wasn't nothing?

Hadley's lungs began to constrict as the panic took hold. There was simply no way she could go back out there and act normal through this dinner without knowing for sure.

Surging to her feet, she snagged one of the tests from the box and ripped it open, following the instructions on the insert with fumbling fingers. She didn't think. She didn't pray. She barely even breathed as she stared at the second hand on her watch, ticking in what felt like an endless circle. Once. Twice. Three times.

Then she looked.

Two bold pink lines showed in the little window.

She simply folded, like a puppet with cut strings, collapsing in a heap on the floor.

Oh God. Oh God! This can't be happening. What are we going to do? What am I going to do?

As the room seemed to close in around her, she pulled her knees into her chest and tried to hang on to her breath.

The knock on the bathroom door nearly made her scream.

"Hadley? Is everything okay?"

Cayla.

Did she lock the door? Shit, if her sister-in-law came in, she'd see, and then Holt would find out, and...

Breathe.

Somehow she managed to push out words. "Yeah, everything's fine. Just touching up my face."

With what makeup bag, Hadley?

But her voice didn't come out sounding like someone had her by the throat, which was a minor miracle.

"Okay, just checking. Dinner's coming off the grill."

"Be right there."

As her footsteps faded, Hadley dragged herself to her feet. She *had* to get herself under control. Wrapping the pregnancy test in toilet paper, she shoved it to the bottom of the bathroom trash can, hiding the evidence. Then she rinsed out her mouth and pinched her cheeks to bring some color back into it. If her eyes looked a little crazed, well, hopefully nobody would look too closely.

It was fine. Everything was going to be fine. No one had to know anything right now. She just had to get through tonight, and then she could be alone to *think*. Except there was Cash.

God, what was he going to say?

Nope. Not gonna think about that now. Can't even consider it. I just have to get through the next couple of hours.

Which meant she had to avoid her lover at all costs, because he was totally going to know something was wrong.

"It's fine. Everything is fine." Hearing the panicked edge in her own voice, she plastered on a smile and went to go earn her Oscar.

4

Cash stood beside the fire pit, one point of a semi-circle with the other guys as they listened to the sizzle of the grill. They each had a beer in hand as they split their attention between the flames and the two little girls playing with the dogs in the yard beyond. Cheerful shrieks and laughter reached them as they rolled on the grass, wrestling and being bathed in ecstatic canine kisses.

"She's come a long way," Holt observed.

Brax released a slow exhale. "There is nothing better than the sound of that laugh. Dakota was so damned scared when the social worker brought them to us. I didn't think she'd ever even talk, let alone smile again." He tipped back another swallow of his beer. "I don't want to think about the things she probably saw, because I know from personal experience exactly how bad it can be."

Cash knew Brax and his wife had both been foster kids themselves, and he recognized by the look in the other man's eyes that his situation had been even worse than what he, Holt, and Hadley had experienced. It made him grateful for the family they'd made together.

"She and Duncan are actual siblings?"

"Yeah." Eyes on his foster daughter to make sure she was out of earshot, Brax continued. "When social services was finally able to take them, their mother had ODed, and the man she was living with had locked them both in a closet. They'd been in there for three days."

"Fuckers," Jonah growled.

Hands and jaws clenched, all of them inherently frustrated at not being able to go back in time and protect these kids from the horrors they'd endured. Not a man among them could tolerate the endangerment of innocents.

Holt clapped a hand on his buddy's shoulder. "They're out now, man. That matters."

"Is the father in the picture?" Cash asked.

"No. Well, Duncan's father is in prison. Dakota doesn't even have one listed on her birth certificate. They don't think it was the same father. Either way, it doesn't seem like there's gonna be anybody to fight the adoption proceedings. We're just waiting on the requisite observation period to count down."

These kids would be safe now. Cash knew Brax and Mia would walk through fire to make sure of it. It was good to know those kinds of people existed in the world. He lifted his longneck. "A toast. To your official, impending parenthood."

"I'll drink to that." Brax clinked his bottle to everyone else's. "It's been a hell of a year. Reconciling with my wife, opening a new business with all of you, renovating the house, and now taking on two kids. Never knew I'd want this so damn much."

"To settling down and finding the one," Jonah added.

Holt grinned. "Wedding planning is making you a sap."

"Wedding planning is making my fiancée a sap, which is very, *very* good for me." He waggled his dark brows before turning sharp green eyes to Cash. "What about you?"

Years of training were the only thing keeping him from jolting. "Me?"

"Yeah. You've been out of the Army for a while, too, right? When are you gonna work on finding your forever girl?"

Was there something else in the tone? The expression? Cash held Jonah's gaze, wondering if his bride-to-be had gone back on her word and told him. But he saw nothing there but good-humored teasing.

To buy himself time, he took another pull on his beer and resisted the urge to look toward the house. He knew Hadley had arrived a little while ago. She hadn't been out to see him. Of course she hadn't. They were still keeping things on the down low. There was absolutely no reason for him to feel disappointed when he'd seen her at the inn right before he drove over. He just wanted this over and done so he could stop squashing all his urges to touch and claim her.

Maybe this conversational gambit was an opening. An opportunity to prime Holt for the idea that he was seriously involved with someone and thinking about forever. But if he did, Holt probably wouldn't rest until he'd ferreted out who, and that circled back to the whole issue of him getting blind-sided in front of a group. Not the best tactic.

Holt lifted the top off the grill. "Cash is too busy snapping up government contracts and recruiting operatives for his private security business."

He wasn't wrong, but he wasn't right, either. The firm was doing just fine. Cash had certainly still found time to fall for Hadley. And if he'd pulled back to more of a directorial role so he stayed closer to home and to her, well, he was the fucking head of Vigilans. It was his company. Others were more interested in continuing to be out in the field than he was. He was happy to be the brains behind the operation and let them.

Holt's remark and the chicken coming off the grill seemed to turn interest away from his love life. By tacit agreement, they began organizing for the rest of the meal. Brax called Dakota and Maddie. Jonah let the women know the chicken was done.

They all fell into a rhythm, corralling dogs, getting little kid hands washed, seeing that the side dishes were brought out to the big picnic table and secondary card table set up for the overflow. Cash turned on the outdoor heater. For all that Tennessee days were still pretty warm in November, now that the sun was well down, the night was more than chilly.

Everyone found a seat. Hadley didn't acknowledge him at all beyond the jerk of her chin as she moved to take a seat at the card table by Maddie. He knew she adored her niece, but it felt almost like a slight, as if she were aiming for the farthest seat away from him. Plates were passed and filled, and conversation began anew around the feeding of kids and fending off of dogs.

"I can't wait for the wedding to be over," Rachel sighed.

"When is it?" Hadley asked.

"In January, after the holidays. God willing, Otis will be fully house-trained by then, since Rebecca volunteered to take him while we're on our honeymoon."

Jonah tweaked the ends of Rachel's long blonde hair. "You and I both know she's eager to do anything that facilitates the production of another grandchild."

"I'd just as soon not think about your mother thinking about our love life." But the look of heat they exchanged made it clear that the idea of starting a family was high on their priority list. And with both of them in their mid-thirties, that made sense. Ticking biological clocks and all that.

"I think these two granted you at least a little reprieve." Mia dropped a kiss to Duncan's head as she fed him more roasted potatoes. He'd been a total Velcro-Boy the whole night, and Mia seemed entirely content with that state of affairs. "She's loving the role of adopted grandma."

Cash already knew Holt was enthusiastic about expanding his brood. Everybody here was settling down into this new kind of life. He felt weird about it. Not like he wanted to be out there on missions anymore, doing crazy shit. He had teams for that.

But this odd little slice of domesticity was worlds away from his reality in Baltimore. Yeah, he wanted a life and a marriage with Hadley, but was this what it would look like? Kids and pets and weeknight cookouts? He couldn't quite wrap his brain around it.

As conversation continued on around him, he glanced toward Hadley. She'd barely touched her food, and though she'd engaged in the chit-chat—mostly focused on the two girls at her table—something felt off. Was she feeling sick again? She'd seemed totally fine, if still a little groggy, when she woke from her nap. That made total sense after the spa treatments he'd talked her into this afternoon, while he caught up on work that couldn't wait. The whole point had been relaxation. But she didn't seem relaxed now. He recognized a vibrating tension in her movements. Maybe it was just anxiety, worried about the prospective confrontation with her brother. She was as eager as he to get it over with. It was almost enough to make him throw caution to the wind and blurt everything out.

Almost.

But that wasn't the way. He'd bide his time. And when they got back to the inn, he'd do whatever he could to reassure her that everything was all going to be okay.

DINNER WAS, blessedly, nearly over. Hadley had managed to finish her meal without a repeat of the nausea. She'd kept most of her interactions focused on Maddie and Dakota. Sweet and engaging little girls, neither of them were old enough to pick up that something was wrong. Everyone else seemed too focused on talk of wedding and adoptions and family to pay much attention to her.

Except for Cash, who was being... Cash. Nothing in his neutral expression gave anything away. She only knew that he knew something was off because she'd had a lifetime to learn how to read him. He hadn't missed the fact that she was avoiding him, but it couldn't be helped. Her capacity to deal with disasters was completely maxed out at the moment.

She didn't know what the hell she was going to say when they got back to the inn, but that was a problem for Future Hadley. Present Hadley was living minute-to-minute. Present Hadley was probably going to be in control for a while.

Cayla clapped her hands. "Okay, everybody grab your plates. We're gonna get everything cleaned up."

The rest of the group moved as one, clearly accustomed to this routine. Hadley instinctively wanted to stick to the rear, but that might give Cash an opportunity to corner her. Instead, she herded the girls into the house and toward the waiting garbage can. They each tossed their paper plate into the trash.

"Good job!" She offered them a high five for the effort before slipping into the stream of people going in and out, grabbing the remaining dishes, utensils, and other detritus from the meal.

The tiny kitchen was packed as adults worked to load dirty platters and casserole dishes into the dishwasher. The dogs danced in and out of legs, playing what seemed to be a game of hide-and-seek or peek-a-boo. Spotting greasy hands about to reach for fur, Hadley grabbed Maddie around the waist, boosting her up.

"Let's get our hands washed. You, too, Dakota."

She held them up to the kitchen faucet one at a time so they could wash their hands. Dakota's feet were dangling when Holt's voice boomed from the back of the house, startling them all.

"B.B., come back here! What is in your mouth? Somebody grab her."

People leapt into motion at the order. Banana Bread streaked through the house, something clutched in her teeth.

She was a blur of golden brown fur as she dodged from person to person, the manic metronome of her tail waving as everyone got in on the game of keep away. Otis and Leno hampered the proceedings, trying to join in themselves. Brax took a header over the pit bull and nearly crashed into a wall. Rachel ended up on her ass, with Otis trying to climb on her head. The girls laughed, and poor Duncan, who'd only just let go of Mia, tried to climb her leg with a wail.

"Gotcha!" Holt managed to snag B.B.'s collar, dragging her to a stop. "Drop it! Drop it! Give it to me."

At last, she relinquished her grip on the thing in her mouth.

Holt examined his prize, his expression turning amused, then lighting up with wonder as he let the dog go and straightened to his full height. Smile wide and delighted, he looked at his wife. "When were you going to tell me?"

Face blank with confusion, Cayla shook her head. "Tell you what?"

He held up the mangled white stick. The positive pregnancy test.

The bottom dropped out of Hadley's stomach again. Unless there was miraculously another one in the bathroom trash—which didn't seem likely—she was about to get outed in front of everybody.

Oh, dear God.

Nobody was focused on her, and she took the opportunity to try to slow her racing pulse, resisting the urge to curl her hands or cross her arms or do anything that might pull attention her way.

Breathe. You have to keep breathing.

"Ah." Cayla's face softened as she stepped up to pat his cheek, the gesture one of intimacy and easy affection. "No. That's why you never look outside the processing window. It'll look like a false positive from the evaporation line. Not pregnant."

Holt's face fell, his big shoulders slumping in disappointment. "Oh."

Wrapping her arms around him, Cayla rose to her toes and brushed her lips to his. "It'll happen. You just have to be patient."

Cayla had covered for her. Relief took all the starch out of Hadley's knees, and she had to put a hand on the lip of the sink to keep from dropping. That wouldn't be the end of it, she was sure, but it wouldn't be coming out here and now before she'd had time to think.

Holt pulled his wife closer, whispering something in her ear that had her cheeks going pink. Twenty bucks said it was a creative suggestion about the next way they should try for that positive. The whole moment was sweet. They'd so clearly be ecstatic to be pregnant and expanding their family. They wanted to have that physical manifestation of their love and commitment. From all indicators, they were putting a lot of time and effort into trying for it on purpose. That was how it should be.

So why the hell couldn't this have happened to *them?*

Hadley needed to get out of here before this curdling anxiety forced her dinner back up and exposed her as Cayla hadn't.

Excitement over, everybody turned back toward post-dinner cleanup. Excuses were being made.

"We need to get the kids on home for bed," Mia said.

"Yeah, we aren't far from bath-time here," Holt added.

Hadley helped round up toys and dogs as an excuse to keep avoiding Cash. She managed to hold her shit together long enough to go hug her brother.

"I'm gonna get on out of here. My car's blocking people in. Thanks for dinner."

He squeezed her back. "See you tomorrow, Squirt."

"Sure. Night, Jerkface."

She made a beeline for the door as Mia and Brax scooped up their kids.

Cayla caught her on the stoop. "Thanks so much for coming. I'm so excited to get to spend more time with you." She pulled Hadley into a hug and whispered, "I'm here if you want to talk."

Well, if she'd needed confirmation that her sister-in-law knew, that was it.

Swallowing hard, Hadley pulled back, daring to look Cayla in the eyes. She saw nothing but compassion and understanding in that gaze. The support for whatever was needed had her control wavering, so she just nodded and headed for her car, feeling as if her world was crumbling down around her ears.

5

Torn between going after Hadley to see what was wrong, and sticking around to deal with this once and for all without her, Cash elected to stay. She needed this resolved. So did he. So he was the one still in the kitchen wiping down counters after everyone else had left and Cayla had hustled Maddie into the bath.

Holt strode in. "You didn't have to do that, man."

"It was nothing. The least I could do for being included."

"Of course you were included. You're family." He clapped Cash on the back as he had so many times before. "That said, I hope you'll understand when I say you've got to go."

"Sorry?"

That hand clamped on his shoulder and began to steer him toward the door. "It's not that I don't want to see you, man. But all the excitement means that Maddie's going to be out like a light. That's a rare enough occurrence that we have to take advantage, if you know what I mean."

He was being given the bum's rush so Holt could go work on turning that negative pregnancy test into a positive. Being a cock blocker was hardly going to help his case, so he conceded defeat yet again.

"Uh... Right. You two have fun with that."

His buddy grinned. "So much fun. God, I love being married. See you tomorrow!"

"Sure. Tomorrow." Cash stepped out onto the stoop and found the door shut smartly behind him.

Well, okay then.

Nothing about this trip was going the way he'd planned. And why should it? It really *hadn't* been planned at all, which was entirely unlike him. He was a man who valued routine and schedules. One who took weeks or months to plan an op. That attention to detail meant he had one of the most successful mission records in the past several decades. But regardless of his personal inclinations, he'd been trained by both life and Uncle Sam how to pivot when necessary. This was just another of those moments. And it meant he had the rest of the night to figure out what was going on with Hadley.

He managed to avoid any of the inn's staff as he made his way upstairs to the third-floor turret room. Not hard this time of night. They'd be getting their own kids down for bed and likely heading that way themselves soon. At the top of the stairs, he paused, listening for signs of anyone else on this level. It seemed no other guests had been added since they'd left for dinner.

Cash unlocked the room and stepped inside. Hadley wasn't in view, but a trail of her clothes started at the foot of the bed and led toward the partially cracked door of the bathroom. Interest piquing, he followed the trail, compulsively scooping up the sweater, jeans, and the lacy red bra that was one of his favorites. The tiny bikini cut briefs that matched were just at the threshold.

Oh, she wasn't playing fair.

Curling his fingers into the fabric, Cash nudged open the door. "Hadley?"

And there she was, hair twisted into a knot, head tipped back as she lounged in the clawfoot tub. There were no bubbles, nothing to hide the body he'd learned so well over these past months. Her skin was flushed pink and rosy from the heat, a contrast to the ink swirling down her arms and around her torso. The sight of the water lapping just above her taut nipples had his cock stirring and all his good intentions wavering, as she'd no doubt intended. He managed some inarticulate noise, unable to stop his gaze from traveling lower, to the dark juncture between her thighs.

She opened those sharp gray eyes and smiled in invitation. "There's room for two."

Only if those two were tightly entwined.

Images of him taking her place lounging as she straddled his lap and rode him to both their pleasure had his nostrils flaring. He took a step forward before he stopped himself.

"We talked about this." He'd put the kibosh on any more intimate activities until he could sort things with her brother.

"I thought that was only because we weren't on the same page about telling Holt. I agree with you about the necessity of it now. But clearly that's going to take a while. Are you really going to deny us what we both want in the meantime?"

He swallowed. "This wasn't why I came in here."

"No?" She glanced pointedly down at the clothes in his hands.

Cash realized he was stroking his fingers over the lace of the underwear as if it were the skin he craved. He fisted his hands. "I wanted to ask if you were okay. You seemed off at dinner."

Something flickered in her eyes before she turned her lips down in a pout. "I hated dinner. Hated that everyone there was free to be open and affectionate, and we weren't. So I stayed away to avoid temptation."

It was a rational explanation, one that echoed his own feelings on the subject. "So you're okay?"

"I will be as soon as you're over here and inside me. Don't make me wait, Cash." She crooked a finger, and he was toast, all his noble intentions washed away under a tsunami of lust.

Fuck it.

He dropped her clothes and began stripping his own.

The water was still only a few shades from scalding when he stepped into it. He lowered himself down on the opposite end of the tub, grateful the faucet apparatus had been mounted to the side instead of the end. Hadley's legs brushed his as she levered herself up and began knee-walking up the length of his body. She was his every fantasy come to life as she braced her hands on his shoulders and positioned herself over his erection, those gloriously tempting breasts right on level with his mouth.

Banding one arm behind her back to draw her close, he curled his tongue around one tight peak. She arched into him on a groan of pleasure, sinking down, down, taking him in with aching slowness, until he was seated as deep as he could go. It was his turn to groan, gripping her hips as he thrust his own, trying for just a little more.

She moaned his name, took his mouth in a slow, searing kiss as she began to move, a slow, lazy ride that let him feel every quiver and pulse of her perfect, wet heat. She so often raced for the finish line, eager to leap off the cliff. But this was different. Tender. Deliberate. As if she wanted to commit every languid second to memory. And it was so damned good. The trust. The intimacy of having nothing between them. Thank God for pharmaceutical birth control.

Feeling her rhythm hitch, her pace quicken, he moved his hands to her breasts, kneading them exactly as he knew she liked. Her breath caught, her movements edging closer to frantic as she chased her release. He watched her ride him, felt her fingers clench his shoulders for purchase. She was a goddess like this, with her skin flushed and her lips swollen, eyes blurred with pleasure. Absolutely breathtaking.

A buzz gathered at the base of his spine. He wouldn't last much longer. Reaching between them, he gently circled her clit, stroking and pressing until she cried out, her body spasming around him hard enough to spark his own release. His arms tightened around her as she fisted around him, and they both came in what felt like an endless wave.

Later, a long time later, she lay slumped against him, limp and sated, her face pressed against his throat. The water was cool, bordering on outright cold. He should get them out and dried off. Bundle her into bed. But he was still buried inside her heat, and he found himself reluctant to move and interrupt this moment of perfect post-coital bliss.

Turning his head, he kissed her shoulder.

Hadley hummed a sleepy note of acknowledgment.

"Feel better?"

She hummed again, burrowing closer.

Smiling to himself, he accepted the need for self sacrifice and maneuvered her off his lap until he could haul them both out of the tub. This was one of those times he was grateful she was such a little thing. He managed to step out without maiming himself and got them both more or less wrapped in towels. The rest of the bathroom cleanup could wait until morning. He needed to get his woman to bed.

Slipping out while Cash was on a conference call was dirty. Maybe not quite as dirty as distracting him with sex last night, so he'd forget to ask any questions. Hadley figured those would be the least of the things she'd need to apologize for before all this was over. And anyway, she'd left him a note instead of straight up disappearing. That ought to count for something. She'd even told him where she was going, if not why.

She'd woken to a text from Cayla saying she'd be at her office all morning if Hadley wanted to come by. There was no intimation that she'd be spilling secrets if Hadley chose otherwise, but Hadley was too afraid not to go. Besides, the nausea was back, and she wouldn't be able to push Cash off again without giving him the truth. She couldn't yet call it what it was. That would make this whole terrible situation that much more real. She wanted a little while longer before she was forced to face the music.

Feeling two steps away from unraveling, Hadley parked in front of the little house where Cayla ran her event planning business. Wiping clammy palms on her jeans, she stepped out of the car and made the gallows walk onto the porch. The door was unlocked. Sucking in a bracing breath, she opened it and went inside. The door opened into what was basically a small, open-concept living room, with a kitchenette tucked off to one side. A sideboard with business cards and wedding magazines sat against the wall of the entryway, and there were shelves displaying a variety of containers, probably as options for centerpieces. A large dining table with chairs occupied much of the space beside the front window. Half of one wall was covered with a marker board. Scrawled lists and post-it notes filled much of the smooth surface. It was a warm, cozy space, just like the woman who'd designed it.

"Cayla?"

"Back here!" She emerged from a short hallway that dog-legged off the main room, taking Hadley in at a glance. "You look terrible."

Hadley grimaced. "Thanks."

"I've got something that will help." Crossing to the kitchenette, she tugged open the fridge and pulled out a pitcher. "I lived on this stuff for the first three or four months I was pregnant with Maddie. It'll help with the morning sickness."

The words hit Hadley like a brick. She'd said it out loud. Pregnant. Morning sickness.

Wheezing a little, she sank down into a chair at the table and dropped her head between her knees. "I kept hoping I'd wake up and it would all be a bad dream."

The pitcher thunked on the table and the next chair dragged out. Cayla's gentle hand fell to her shoulder. "I'm guessing this was not planned."

The hysteria she'd been holding back since last night bubbled up in the form of a hyena's laugh. "Planned? To get knocked up when my business has only barely stayed consistently in the black for eight months? When we're still so damned new? No, this was definitely not planned."

She could just imagine how Cash would approach planning a pregnancy. He'd research the hell out of it, have reams of data, and write some kind of computer program that would spit out the optimal time and position for impregnation. He'd have every detail figured out, down to the minute, because he was that thorough. Okay, that was unfair. It made him sound robotic and clinical, and he was anything but as a lover. But all those characteristics were why he was good at his job, why he was one of the most sought after assets in his field. And she'd so loved shaking him out of that rigidity, knowing she could make him forget it all. But she'd never wanted to do it like this.

All the fear and anger and frustration spilled out as she straightened. "This is going to ruin everything. I'm not ready for this. I don't even know if I *want* kids."

Cayla squeezed her shoulder and poured a glass of whatever was in the pitcher. "I can assure you, nobody's ever ready, even when you do want kids and are actively trying. Nine months seems like forever and no time at all. But we'll be here for you every step of the way, no matter what."

Hadley sat back, stunned at the jump. Then it occurred to her that Tennessee was one of the states where women had no options or rights to bodily autonomy. Thank God she lived in Maryland and had choices. Not that choice made this any easier. "It was never supposed to get serious between us, and we sure as hell never talked about the possibility of kids."

"Are you afraid he won't stand by you?"

"No." The denial was instant and absolutely certain. "I know he will. But I don't want to trap him. I don't want him to resent me. And I sure as fuck don't want to end up in some kind of toxic replay of what my mother lived."

Short of ending up out on the streets, Hadley couldn't imagine a fate worse than that.

Cayla's empathetic expression shifted to no-nonsense. "First off, calm down. That's never going to happen. You aren't your mama. Holt raised you better than that. Second, does Cash know?"

All the blood drained out of her head. "Is it that obvious?"

A faint hint of amusement lit her brown eyes. "I've suspected for a while."

A fresh spate of panic shot through her. "Does Holt know?"

"No. I figured that was best coming from y'all, even before this."

On a slow breath, she picked up the glass Cayla had poured and began to sip. The smooth lemon-lime flavor slid down her throat, almost immediately soothing her stomach. "What is this, anyway?"

"It's kind of like a lemon-limeade. Tons of fresh lemon and lime juice, mixed with a simple syrup."

"It's good. And I think it's already helping."

"Getting some food in there will probably help, too. Have you had breakfast?"

"I couldn't tolerate the thought of it."

Her sister-in-law retrieved some saltine crackers. "I don't have a ton here, but give these a try."

Hadley opened a sleeve and began to nibble. "I'm the reason we didn't tell Holt we were involved to begin with. I figured he'd freak out, and I didn't think it was any of his business if we decided to scratch each other's itch."

"Mmm. And how long has said itch-scratching been going on?"

"Six months. Even before... well... this, things were getting more serious than we planned. Cash had a crisis of conscience about the whole thing. It's why we both came down, planning to tell Holt in our own way. But this changes everything."

"Does it?" Cayla challenged.

"How can it not? Now it's not just a matter of explaining to my brother, 'Oh, hey, we're hot for each other. By the way, we epically fucked up.' I don't know if he would've lost his shit over us seeing each other, but he will absolutely lose his shit over this." She grabbed Cayla's hand. "You can't tell him."

Cayla offered a reassuring squeeze. "I swear, I won't. I covered for you last night, and I'll keep covering for you as long as you need. But you have to talk to Cash. He needs to be in on this whole decision. Whatever that decision ends up being. Then you both need to talk to Holt about the two of you. Together. I get why you waited, but he's going to be hurt that you didn't trust him."

"Yeah, well, he's the least of my worries right now." Hadley ate another cracker and poured another glass of the magic anti-nausea drink. "I need to get my head on straight before I talk to Cash. Can I hang out here for a while?"

"Of course. You stay as long as you need. I meant what I said. We're here for you, no matter what. That's what family does."

It wasn't what all families did, but it was clear Cayla meant it.

Hadley leaned forward and wrapped her in a hug. "I'm really glad my brother married you."

Cayla squeezed her back. "Me, too, honey. Me, too."

6

H adley had snuck out on him.

Okay, maybe that wasn't entirely fair. She'd left a note, and he had been tied up on a conference call with part of his team for the better part of an hour. But she'd made no effort to actually see him before she slipped out to go hang with Cayla. Not that she needed to check in with him. They'd come to Eden's Ridge separately, regardless of the fact that she'd found her way back into his bed. But something about her actions smacked of avoiding him. After the intensity of last night, he didn't like it.

As she had every right to spend time with her sister-in-law, Cash packed up his laptop and headed to Bad Boy Bakers. He didn't actually figure he'd get an opportunity to talk to Holt while he was at work, but the bakery was across the street from Cayla's office, so he'd be able to tell when Hadley finished up there.

Because business seemed to be jumping this morning, Cash bypassed the line and secured one of the four-top tables. None of them had a direct line of sight across the street, but beggars couldn't be choosers. It wasn't like he was conducting actual surveillance. He was just pulling out his computer when Holt strode over.

"Using us as your office today?"

"Might as well. It's a change of scenery from the inn."

Holt winced. "I'm sorry we haven't gotten to spend much time together since you got here."

"Man, it's fine. Your life is different now with the business and your family. You can't just pick up and do shit anymore. That's what I get for going with impulse instead of planning."

"When do you have to head back to Baltimore?"

Cash mentally flipped through his schedule. "I definitely have to be back by Monday. I can work remotely in the meantime."

"I'm kinda slammed this week, prepping for various events, but I'll be done by dinner tomorrow. We'll have a big family deal, and then I'm all yours on Saturday."

He could sit on this news one more day if he had to. "Sounds good."

"You had breakfast?"

"Like three hours ago." Which, come to think of it, was wearing off.

"I'll bring you something to tide you over."

"Appreciate it."

Cash had his laptop open and his own mobile network set up by the time Holt brought back a cup of coffee and an everything bagel smeared with cream cheese. Taking a sip of the rich black brew, he nodded his thanks and immersed himself into computer code, building a virus his team would need for a mission next month.

Customers came and went, and the guys seemed to rotate out who was manning the front. Cash paid them little heed until he heard a deep voice.

"Actually, I'm looking for someone. Is Jonah Ferguson here?"

There was an authority in the tone that had him looking up, his instincts twanging. The guy was dressed as a civilian, in jeans and boots, with broad shoulders filling out a leather jacket. His hair was a mix of dark and silver, with a short, mostly silver beard highlighting what Cash could see of his face. His stance was easy, but Cash recognized the self-possession of someone who could handle himself. He'd lay money this guy was career military.

The kitchen door swung open, and Jonah stepped out, wiping his hands on a towel. "Hey, are we nearly out of something up here? Because I've got some—" His eyes landed on the stranger, and the towel fell from his fingers as he snapped to immediate attention, lifting his hand in a salute. "Sir."

Well, that confirmed his assumption.

The man's mouth twitched. "At ease, Sailor."

Jonah skirted around the counter and offered a hand. The guy took it, pulling him into a back-slapping hug that proved he had some deeper relationship with Jonah than that of a superior.

Either way, it was clear he hadn't been expected.

"Not that it isn't good to see you, Captain. But what are you doing here?"

Captain. Ah. One of Jonah's former commanding officers?

"Well, you're not the only one who retired. I heard what you'd been up to and wanted to come check on you." When Jonah didn't immediately respond to that, the guy shoved his hands into the pockets of his leather jacket. "How are you doing?"

Jonah grinned. "I'm great. I'm getting married."

"That's wonderful."

The two slipped into small talk, and Cash turned his focus back to his work. At least until the bell over the door jangled, and a woman's voice rang out. "Hey, Baby. Do you have my order ready?"

Something in the air changed, sharpening Cash's focus.

Jonah called out, "Sure, Mom. It's in the back. I'll get it in just a minute."

The new guy turned toward Jonah's mother, Rebecca. As she caught sight of him, her eyes widened and her mouth fell open.

He grinned, and suddenly there was a touch of East Tennessee drawl in his voice. "Hey, Rebel. It's good to see you."

So much flickered over her face before she rushed over to wrap him in a hug. "Oh, my God. What are you doing here?"

He hugged her back, and Cash didn't miss the old intimacy in the gesture. "I came to check on your boy, to see how he's doing now that he's retired."

She pulled back, blinking in surprise. "You know my son?"

He seemed to consider his reply. "I was his commanding officer for a number of years."

Rebecca paled.

Why should that be an issue?

"How did you know he was mine?"

The captain laughed. "It was impossible not to. You stamped yourself all over his face. And, of course, he's a Ferguson."

Jonah cleared his throat. "I'm sorry. What the hell is happening here? You two know each other?"

Cash could read the struggle between respect for his CO and the desire to protect his mother.

Rebecca laid a hand on the captain's shoulder. "This is Grey."

Jonah turned disbelieving eyes on Grey. "*You?* You used to be skinny as a rail and have a *ponytail?*"

Yeah, the man had military written all over him. Cash couldn't see it either.

"He saw some pictures of us from back in high school recently," Rebecca explained.

"I did have a life before the Navy."

At the statement, she stiffened, her hand falling away. Some kind of history there. One Cash was banking that Jonah didn't know.

Rebecca turned her attention back to her son. "Baby, if you can get my order. I really need to get going. I'm gonna be late."

Jonah hesitated, clearly trying to decide what all this meant, but ultimately, he nodded and headed back into the kitchen.

A shield was up in his mother's expression when she turned back to the visitor. "Well, it's been great to see you, Grey. I'm glad to know you're doing well."

"I'm retired, actually."

"Oh?" Jonah's mom definitely didn't need to play poker. A blind man could've seen the interest there. Or maybe that was just Cash, with all his training in how to read body language.

"Yeah."

Jonah emerged, handing over a box. "Here you go."

She kissed his cheek. "Thanks, sweetie." Her eyes drifted back to Grey as she turned toward the door. "I've gotta go. You take care."

"Will do. And I'll be seeing you around, Rebel."

Her steps stuttered at the unmistakable promise in his voice.

"I figure it's high time I looked at moving home."

Rebecca made her escape without another word.

Cash wondered if there was any popcorn in the back, because this was the most entertainment he'd had in a while. Clearly there was some kind of history between Jonah's mom and his former CO. History that predated Jonah, if they'd gone to high school together.

All the warmth had left Jonah's expression. "With all due respect, sir, how is it in all these years you never saw fit to mention you were from my hometown, and you knew my mother?"

Grey's posture shifted. It was a subtle move, but one that unquestionably indicated he was back in the role of CO again. "It was need-to-know information, and you didn't need to know. Glad you're doing well, Ferguson. I'm sure I'll see you again."

He strode out without another word.

Immediately, the other patrons that had gone silent during the exchange pulled out phones and began to text. Whatever that was would be all over town by the end of business today.

"What the actual hell?" Jonah muttered.

Cash had suspicions, but before he could decide whether to share any of them, his phone vibrated with a text.

Hadley: **Meet me back at the inn?**

He fired off a quick reply that he was en route and packed up his stuff. Whatever was going on with Jonah's shit could wait. Hadley was his priority.

HADLEY PACED the confines of their turret room at The Misfit Inn, feeling like a caged animal. She'd gone over and over the whole thing in her head, trying to find the right words, the right way to admit this to Cash that wouldn't destroy who they were to each other. She'd gotten involved with him in the first place because she'd believed they could cross that line into more, then go back to being the friends they'd always been. The idea of losing him had never entered her mind.

But it had taken root now and brought to light the thing she'd been in denial about for months.

She was in love with Cash.

Maybe a part of her always had been. But what she'd found with him was so much more than her naïve teenaged self had imagined. He accepted her for who she was, utterly and completely. As someone who'd so often been told she was too much, being someone's just right was an incredibly precious gift. But that just right didn't include an unplanned baby, and Hadley was absolutely terrified this would change how he looked at her. That it would change who they were to each other.

Oh, if she chose to go through with this, he'd stand by her. She knew that. He'd give all the support she and a child needed because he knew what it was to be without. But what if this baby meant *she* stopped mattering? That was how a lot of people saw it. That the moment another life was made, the mother ceased to exist as a person. She was an incubator, and her dreams, her everything, were supposed to be put on the back burner for the sake of the child, because that was what a "good" woman did.

If Cash believed that, it was going to absolutely break her heart.

Overwhelmed, she dropped into the chair at the little writing desk, pulling her feet onto the seat and wrapping her arms around her knees, as if the position would protect her from what was to come. She'd done this so often as a child, in her room, in closets, wherever she and Holt had hidden to get away from the fights between their mother and her latest disappointment of a boyfriend, or the emotional tantrums she threw when they left and she fell into a bottle. But her brother wasn't here to protect her now. He didn't have an arm around her and wasn't singing an endless parade of Disney tunes and Broadway musicals to distract her. She had to face this alone.

Alone was fucking terrifying.

It wasn't that Cash would rage. That wasn't his way. But this would change them, and she'd only just realized she desperately wanted to keep the them they'd become.

At the sound of the knob, Hadley tightened her hold on her legs and sent up a silent prayer that she didn't somehow make this worse than it already was.

Cash stepped into the room, his gaze moving unerringly to her. His brows drew together in instant concern, and she could see him shifting into action mode, already striding toward her.

"What's wrong?"

Hadley held up a hand to stay him. She wanted his comfort almost more than her next breath, but she didn't think she could get through this if he touched her. And a part of her wasn't sure she deserved that comfort.

He stopped two steps away, that groove between his brows deepening. "Hadley?"

"It was mine." She blurted it out. And damn it, that wasn't how she'd meant to begin. But the fear was multiplying like ants in her chest, and she had to let it out somehow.

"What was yours?"

"The pregnancy test."

He stared at her, his big brain clearly not processing that.

"The one the dog had last night." She closed her eyes. "It... wasn't an evaporation line."

"You're pregnant?" There was only the faintest rising of his tone, which, in Cash-speak, was pure shock.

Hadley nodded, struggling to hold back the flood of tears that wanted to fall. She had no doubt there'd be many, but she needed to get through this first.

Bracing herself, she met his gaze head-on. "I didn't do this on purpose." It seemed absolutely vital to establish that, as they both knew women around them where they grew up who'd done that.

"I know you didn't." The absolute certainty in the statement had some of the knots in her stomach unraveling.

Moving slowly, as if he thought she might spook, he closed the distance between them, gripping the arms of the chair to pull it over to the bed. Then he sat and gently pried one of her hands free to fold into his. That simple gesture all but undid her because he wasn't pushing her away.

"Okay. How do you want to handle it?"

She blinked at him. "You're not going to make declarations?"

"No." His tone was low and soft, and she had the impression he was treating her like a bomb that could go off at any moment. It wasn't an inaccurate comparison. "I can express my opinion, but it's your body, your choice. I'd rather know how you feel about it before I get into my thoughts."

"I don't even know how I feel. I swore I'd never let this happen again."

He was good at shielding his emotions, but not good enough to cover the tremor that went through him at the statement. "Again?"

This was the part she feared the most. Admitting her truth and not knowing how he'd react. Swallowing hard, she curled tighter against her knees.

"After Holt went into the Army and I was out on my own, I got involved with this guy. I was careful. He... was not. When I turned up pregnant, he bailed. There was a part of me that was glad of that, because I knew getting married because of a baby was a terrible idea. That was how it started with my parents before my dad walked. Better he show his true colors before going down that path." She sucked in a breath, wishing it did anything to calm her.

"I knew what it was to be raised by a single parent who couldn't hack it. I was eighteen. No education yet. No career. I was barely supporting myself. I sure couldn't support a child. I had no one. Holt had only just gotten free of raising me, and I wasn't about to ask him to help again. Plus, I'm pretty sure he'd have killed the guy. Add to that, I kept thinking of you."

"Me?"

"I had a front-row seat to how awful it was on you to be raised by a mother who resented you, who wasn't ready to be a parent, who didn't want you and took every opportunity to say so. I wasn't ready. I didn't want that child. Didn't want a permanent tie with a guy who wasn't going to stand by me. There was no reason to expect he'd somehow come back and stand by the child, either. So I got an abortion."

Back then, it hadn't even been a question. There was no other rational alternative. "I'm so fucking thankful that I had the privilege of that. That I lived in a state where it wasn't a question. Where I didn't have to give up my life because of a mistake. A lot of women aren't that lucky. You and I both know that the people behind those rules don't give a good damn about the life of a child once it exits the womb. They don't understand the reality of that hypothetical life. We do because we lived it."

Hadley straightened her shoulders, feeling some defiance in the face of his absolutely unchanged expression. "We lived it," she repeated. "And because we did, I got an abortion. I've never regretted it."

She sat back in the chair, extracting her hand from his as she waited on the backlash for having made that decision, bracing herself for the judgment so many freely gave without knowing anything. It was why she'd never told a soul what she'd done. But now she'd told the man she loved. Her truth was out there, a bomb lying between them. And she was bracing herself for the detonation that would mean the end of them.

7

C ash sat in stunned silence, not willing to speak until he figured out the right thing to say and the best way to handle this so that Hadley was okay. Because, right now, she definitely wasn't.

Despite her fragile show of bravado, she was obviously terrified. Of the situation. Of what he'd say and do. She so clearly believed on some level that he'd judge her for what she'd shared. That he'd think the worst of her. A part of him wanted to be insulted at that, but it was exactly what many people thought when confronted with a story like hers. That it was her fault. Her penance. Purely her responsibility simply for being a woman. As if the guy hadn't had anything to do with it. And that son of a bitch had walked away because there were no rules in place to hold men accountable.

Her choosing to go against that social expectation had to have taken unimaginable strength. And Cash was so fucking glad for her sake that there had been a choice, because having that baby at eighteen would have irrevocably changed her life. Changed her. And who she'd become was amazing.

"Holt doesn't know." That was absolutely certain, because if he had, she was right... the asshole wouldn't still be breathing and Cash would have been the one called to help hide the body.

"No one knew. Except the asshat who bailed. The doctor. And now you."

"Thank you for trusting me with that." It *was* an act of trust. She could've told him about this pregnancy without ever breathing a word of her prior experience.

The ring seemed to pulse in his pocket. He wanted to pull it out and propose right now, but he'd heard what she said about getting married because of a baby being a terrible idea. He didn't want her to think that it was only because of the baby. He loved her. He wanted *her*. And damn it, why hadn't he said so sooner? Would she even believe him now?

Focus. That was a problem for later.

Because he didn't think he could get her hand back without a fight, he curled his fingers around her ankle, wanting to touch her, to give her some kind of comfort.

"You're right that I was one of those unwanted children. I don't know what my mother would've been like if she'd had an option not to have me. Maybe she'd have been better. Happier. I can't unwish my existence, but a big chunk of those years was hell. I know there are some people out there who'd argue that I'm a success story. A reason to choose life. Look at all I've accomplished. But I'm the exception, not the rule. I fought tooth and nail for every fucking thing I have. And I was lucky, having you and Holt. Not everyone is. Hell, based on how all of us grew up, I'd argue most aren't. So, you did the right thing. It makes no logical sense to have a child you didn't want and couldn't afford. It would've destroyed your life." That had been the message beaten into his head on the daily when he'd been young. That he'd been the reason his mother's life was over.

"And none of that is to say I believe you'd do any of the things my mother or yours did if you choose to have this baby.

You know exactly what it's like, and you'd never put a child through that. I actually think you'd be an amazing mother, because of what you went through. But only if you want that for yourself. If you do, I'll be there with you, for both of you, every single step of the way and after. If you don't—either because you're not ready or because you don't want a child with me—" The idea of that hit him in the chest with a pang, but he forged on. "—or at all, that's okay, too. There are options between both those extremes. It's your choice, and I won't force you on this."

Her body shook as the tears spilled over, and Cash couldn't take it anymore. He scooped her out of the chair, hauling her into his lap and wrapping his arms tight around her as she sobbed out her fear and, he hoped, found some relief.

It gave him more of a chance to absorb the news himself. This wasn't some hypothetical potential future like he'd been kicking around this past week. They'd created a child between them. The reality of that struck him like a bullet train. It hadn't been on purpose, but that didn't make it any less meaningful. They'd made a baby, and something deep and visceral responded to that. *Wanted* that.

But what if she didn't? If she was willing to carry to term— and that was a big if—would he be willing to do it on his own? What would he be willing to do as a single dad? It wasn't a question most men asked themselves, probably. Men inherently weren't expected to do what single mothers were all the time. They weren't forced to bring children into the world that they didn't want. Not in the same way as women. And if he made that decision, no doubt people would praise him for being some amazing guy simply for doing the minimum right thing as a parent. The double standard was staggering and disgusting. But it didn't stop him from asking the question. Would he want to raise a kid on his own?

He'd been a child utterly rejected by his biological family.

He never wanted his own child to feel like he had. He wanted to be there for every moment, to make absolutely *certain* his child never felt unwanted. And because of that, he knew he couldn't force this on Hadley. He couldn't force himself on her. It wasn't his right. Even wanting this child, he couldn't very well demand that she carry it to term. As he'd told her, it was her body, her decision. In no universe could he insist she endure a pregnancy and everything that went along with that, physically and emotionally. That wasn't fair or reasonable.

Long after she'd soaked his shirt, Hadley lifted her head to look at him. Those gray eyes looked almost silver behind the sheen of more tears. "I need to know—everything else being equal, what do you want?"

This he didn't have to consider. The answer was simply there.

"I want you. At the beginning, middle, and end of the day, I always want you. I want us. You don't have to decide right this second. It's a lot to think about. And it seems like the first order of business would be finding out how far along you are." They needed to confirm she really was pregnant, and that everything was okay. That it wasn't one of those ectopic pregnancies she'd mentioned, or something else that endangered her health. Then they'd have a better basis for making a decision.

Her face went white. "I can't do that here. It'll get back to Holt."

Yeah, he didn't need to be hearing this news yet.

"Then we'll drive up to Johnson City or down to Knoxville."

She swallowed again, her voice a little tremulous. "You'll go with me?"

Cash combed the hair back from her face, cupping her cheek in his palm. "Every step, Had." Then he gently laid his lips over hers.

～

HADLEY COULDN'T BELIEVE they'd gotten a same day appointment. The Johnson City doctor's office was nice, as such places went. Clean, modern lines, lots of light, and a boatload of floral prints that were probably supposed to be relaxing but didn't override the pervasive scent of antiseptic. The staff appeared to be entirely made up of women, which Hadley appreciated. If she was going to have to wear this absurd paper gown that barely covered her, at least the only guy to take in the show was the one who'd already seen every inch of her.

That guy currently stood sentry by the exam table, blocking her from the sight of anyone who might come into the room. The body language of the gesture betrayed the soldier he'd once been, though he'd inherently been a protector from the beginning. The heart he so carefully shielded would never allow him to walk away from an innocent who couldn't defend themselves. That was one of the things she'd always loved about him, even before she'd fallen for him. There'd been so little safety in her early life. What she'd enjoyed had been entirely because of her brother and because of Cash.

His steady presence was the only thing keeping her from flying apart while she waited, cool air kissing skin she didn't want exposed. She wasn't a prudish woman. She was proud of her body, of the art inked into it. But this made her feel vulnerable. Afraid.

And yet, it was such a vast difference from the last time she'd been in this position. Then she'd been utterly alone in her terror. So very young to be carrying the weight of such a huge decision. She'd meant what she'd told Cash last night. She'd never regretted making that choice. But it had been so very hard in the moment. Even at the clinic where the procedure had been performed, they'd forced her to endure the ultrasound. Made her look at the screen so that the full reality of what she intended was made clear. They'd accepted her decision without argument, given back her freedom. The only cost was the shame and guilt. It had taken her years to work through that. To be comfortable in the certainty that she'd made the right choice, not condemning herself and a child to poverty and struggle.

"Hey." Cash's voice pulled her out of the memory.

He'd circled around in front of her, bracing his hands on either side of her legs on the exam table, caging her in. From anyone else, the move might've been domineering and made her feel claustrophobic. But from Cash, it felt safe. As if he were wrapping that cloak of unflappable calm around her.

"This is just the next logical step. The next piece of data. No decisions have been made. You're still in control here." He followed the assurance with a kiss to her brow.

Hadley couldn't stop herself from reaching for him, cuddling close for a hug. His arms slid around her, warm and solid.

"I'm really glad you're here with me."

His voice rumbled against her ear. "I wouldn't be anywhere else."

A perfunctory knock sounded on the door before it swung open and two women strode in. The darker of the two stepped forward and offered a warm smile. "Hello! I'm Dr. Washington. You must be Ms. Steele and Mr....?"

"Grantham." With one last squeeze, Cash stepped away, nodding to the doctor.

"Nice to meet you." Dr. Washington dropped onto the rolling stool. "Well, let's get right to it then. I'm sure you're eager to have that home pregnancy test confirmed. You are definitely pregnant. Congratulations!"

Hadley swallowed hard and wanted to curl up into a ball. She'd known there wouldn't be a different answer. The morning sickness made that clear enough. But a part of her had hoped.

Cash took her hand.

When neither of them burst into spontaneous joy, Dr. Washington clued in that this wasn't a thing they'd necessarily be celebrating. She sobered, nodding in a brisk, no-nonsense fashion, her velvety brown eyes kind as she rolled over to the foot of the exam table. "Let's get to the physical exam and see what there is to see, and then we'll do the ultrasound to figure out how far along you are."

Right. Now she got to endure a total stranger poking around in her lady parts. Resigned, Hadley fit her feet into the stirrups and leaned back, staring at the blank ceiling.

"I've never understood why we don't have posters of hot guys on the ceiling, so we have something to look at while things are going on down there."

Dr. Washington laughed. "That would make things more bearable, wouldn't it?"

Cash huffed a laugh and kissed the back of her hand.

Through a casual discussion of favorite actors and pretty faces they'd vote for ceiling art, she endured the pelvic exam. When it came time for the ultrasound, she managed not to make a dirty joke at the sight of the transducer—which still totally looked like a dildo. Her eyes stayed resolutely on the ceiling as Dr. Washington did her thing.

"Ah ha, here we are. That right there is the head. And you can see the arm and leg buds just there."

Hadley tensed, blinking back the heat of tears as she kept her gaze firmly above her.

"Wow." Cash's hand tightened on hers, but Hadley didn't think he was aware of it.

She chanced a look at his face and caught the unguarded moment of awe as he stared at the screen. Through this whole thing, he'd been so very careful to keep his emotions battened down, to avoid influencing her decision. But in this moment, faced with the reality of what they'd created, his instinctive reaction wasn't grim resolution, wasn't regret or anger. It was something that might have been joy.

That alone gave her the courage to look for herself.

The shape on the screen looked more like a malformed lima bean to her, but she could see well enough the suggestion of a spine and the bulbous alien head that was almost the same size as the rest of the body. Though it wasn't clear, there was the suggestion of a face in the profile. She couldn't stop herself from wondering if those features would be predominantly her or Cash or some blend of both.

"I'm thinking you're right around eight or nine weeks." Dr. Washington flipped some switch, and the room was filled with a fast swishing sound. "Heartbeat is steady at a good 160 beats per minute."

"So fast," Cash murmured.

"Totally normal at this stage." She pressed a button and the machine spit out a photo of the lima bean. "Baby's first picture."

Hadley's hand shook as she accepted it.

Finished with the exam, the doctor rolled over to the sink to wash her hands. "Everything looks good. You and the fetus are healthy. You'll want to start some prenatal vitamins if you haven't already, and otherwise, follow up with your OB when you get back home. I've got some literature to send home with you. The nurse will have it waiting for you in the hall. Do you have any questions?"

Mute, Hadley could only shake her head.

Dimly, she was aware of Cash thanking the doctor and of being told she could get dressed, but it was mostly white noise. Then they were alone again.

"Do you want me to take it?" His tone was gentle, though his face was back to being that imperturbable mask.

She handed the glossy black-and-white picture to him and slid off the table, half expecting the world to tilt as she did.

"Okay. You're healthy. There's nothing life-threatening that needs to be dealt with immediately. You've got the next piece of information and time to think about what you want to do."

Not bothering to draw the curtain between them, she pulled on her underwear. "You're still not going to say what your opinion is?"

"No. Because my opinion might influence yours, and it's your choice."

But she'd seen his face when he looked at the sonogram, when they'd heard the heartbeat. She knew his opinion. Maybe not on them, but on this. It would hurt him if she chose termination. Turning her back, she continued to dress, thinking about what it had been like to be with him all these months.

He loved her. Had always loved her, on some level. He might not be *in* love with her, but she knew if she opted to continue this pregnancy, she wouldn't be doing it alone. He'd never walk away. Not from her. Not from his child. If she chose to have this baby, it would bind them together forever. Certainly not the way she might've wanted, but maybe it wouldn't be horrible. Maybe it could work.

She had a lot more thinking to do, and she was so incredibly grateful he was letting her run the show. That he'd gone out of his way not to force her hand in any way.

Fully dressed, she crossed the room and took his face in her hands, drawing him down for a soft kiss. "Thank you for being great."

He pressed his brow to hers. "Thank you for being mine."

8

Almost as soon as they returned from Johnson City, Hadley crashed. The whole ordeal had taken a lot out of her. Cash was grateful for the reprieve. Maintaining utter neutrality was sapping his own reserves. He'd meant everything he'd said to her. This was her choice. He'd accept it. He was sticking by her, no matter what.

But seeing their baby on that screen? Damn, he hadn't known that would hit him so hard. It was one thing to talk in the abstract about the idea of kids someday. It was a whole other ballgame, knowing they'd started one. Realizing that, if she went through with this, in less than a year, he'd be holding that child.

He *wanted* that.

More, he wanted her to want that.

But he'd never guilt her into it. In an ideal world, a child should be wanted by both its parents. No kid ought to feel like a burden or a problem or a mistake. She'd never intentionally do that to a child, but if she wasn't really all in to do this, it could very well be expressed in subtle ways. Kids were a hell of a lot more perceptive than adults ever gave them credit for. No, better not to risk it.

If they didn't keep this baby, he'd grieve. But it didn't mean they couldn't have another in the future, when she was more comfortable with the idea. But for that to be a possibility, he had to secure that future, and that meant talking to Holt. There was no more waiting for the perfect time, the perfect spin. He simply had to get it done. Before tonight, in case he took it badly, so Cash had time to do damage control. Holt had said this morning that he'd be staying late prepping cakes for events, so Cash left Hadley sleeping and headed for the bakery.

As it was after two, the front door for customers was locked. He followed the wrap-around porch to the side door leading into the kitchen. Faint strains of—was that *The Greatest Showman?*—sounded from the other side. Cash pulled it open and stepped in, pausing only long enough to verify that Holt had seen him before barking, "Outside. Now," and turning back around.

If this went sideways, no reason for blood to be shed in his workspace. That'd probably be a health code violation. Cash rolled his shoulders, loosening his muscles for a fight, even though he didn't intend to put one up.

A few moments later, Holt strode out, his brows drawn together. "What the hell's going on? What's wrong?"

Knowing this could be the end of his relationship with his friend, his brother, Cash hesitated only a moment. Nothing was more important than Hadley. No matter what decision she made, she was it for him. That was the only thing crystal clear to him.

"Hit me."

"I'm sorry, what?"

"Hit me, and get it out. Get it over with," Cash urged.

Concern shifted to bafflement. "Why would I be hitting you?"

"Because I want to marry your sister."

If ever there'd been a record scratch moment...

Holt's jaw dropped. "Excuse me?"

"I'm in love with Hadley, and I want to marry her."

When his friend continued to stare in absolute shock, Cash filled in the silence. "I've been trying to find the right way, the right time, to tell you for days. Clearly that's not going to happen. I don't have time to wait anymore. So hit me. Let's get it over with so I can get on with my life."

Clearly a little slow on the uptake, Holt shook his head. "I thought you looked at her as a sister."

"I did for a long time. Until I didn't. We've been friends all our lives. We've always had a connection. But we reconnected this year, and it was different."

The bafflement morphed into realization. "You've been dating my sister." Not a question.

Figuring he deserved it, Cash braced himself for a punch. "Yes."

Holt didn't move. "Why didn't you tell me?"

"She didn't want to." Maybe that was chicken shit, blaming her. But it was the truth.

"Why?"

"I'm reasonably sure it involved her being convinced your reaction was going to fall somewhere between planting a fist in my face and burying me in a shallow grave."

Holt angled his head, though whether it was in concession of the point or merely an "Ah," Cash couldn't have said. "So both of you being down here at the same time isn't an accident."

"Yes, and no. I came down to tell you. She followed me, hoping to mitigate the damage. We've both been circling around you for days."

"I see." Holt's expression locked down, and Cash didn't

know what to do with that. He'd have been more comfortable with a beat down or shouting than this stoicism.

He found himself babbling to fill the silence, like some kind of untrained civilian. "Look, man, I love you. You're the closest thing I've got to a brother. But I love her more, and if it comes down to her or you, I'm choosing her. If you need to hit me, I understand. But it won't change anything. I'll still be in love with her."

His brother of the heart sucked in a breath. They both knew the weight of what Cash was saying.

"Is she in love with you?"

She hadn't said the words, but her actions had told him in countless other ways. "God, I hope so, or that ring I bought is going to collect a lot of dust."

The stoic mask cracked, more shock bleeding through. "You already bought a ring?"

"Yeah." Because he didn't think Holt was going to sucker punch him, Cash pulled the box from his pocket and flipped it open. The ruby solitaire was set in platinum and flanked by a row of small diamonds on both sides. It was strong and beautiful. Bold. Like her.

Holt scrubbed a hand on the back of his neck. "Shit. You're serious."

"As a heart attack."

Cash put the ring away and shifted on the balls of his feet, opening himself wide to whatever blow was coming.

When Holt just laid a hand on his shoulder, he flinched. "I'm not going to hit you."

"Shallow grave, then?"

He huffed a laugh. "Not that either. You're one of the best men I know. She'd be lucky to have you. And God knows, you two know each other well enough. You'll be good for each other."

Cash couldn't have heard him right. But Holt just continued to stare at him with level blue eyes.

"You're... okay with this?"

"I mean... it's a little weird. But you're both grown adults. That five-year age difference hardly matters now. You have the right to make your own choices. I'm not gonna complain that two of my favorite people chose each other."

Cash swayed a little as the starch went out of his knees. He wasn't going to lose his brother. They hadn't destroyed their little family by getting romantically involved. None of it was going to be the big upset either of them was worried about. Cash just hoped that remained true if and when Holt found out about the pregnancy.

Holt pulled him in for a back-thumping hug and grinned. "So, when are you gonna give her the ring?"

～

THE MOMENT HADLEY woke to find the room empty, she knew. Cash had gone to talk to her brother. Alone.

Shit!

This wasn't what they'd discussed, but evidently, after today, he'd deemed a solo confrontation worth the risk.

Scrambling out of bed, she fought through the dregs of a coma-level nap to find her jeans. She'd go after him. Maybe she could still get there in time to minimize the damage. She nearly took a header into the desk as she hopped her way into her jeans. Shoes. Where the hell were her shoes? She scanned the floor, certain she'd kicked them off by the bed. At last, she found them tucked neatly under the luggage rack, no doubt placed there by Mr. Neat himself before he went to face execution. Hadley dove for them, dragging one bootie on. The other was in her hand when the door opened.

"Cash!"

Abandoning the other shoe, she flew to him, checking him over for injuries, searching for bruises or blood.

One corner of his mouth kicked up as he wrapped his arms around her. "Hi. I'm happy to see you, too."

His short, dark beard rasped against her palms when she framed his face. "You're not hurt." Her brain was busy trying to catch up to what her eyes were telling her.

"I'm not."

With a long, slow exhale, she slumped against him. "I thought you went to talk to Holt."

"Oh, no—I did. I told him about us."

"And you're still walking?"

He stroked a hand down her spine, soothing. "Believe me, I'm as surprised as you are. I think he was kind of insulted that we thought he'd be angry."

"He came very close to breaking the arm of my prom date for having a condom in his wallet."

"As I was the one who picked said wallet from your prom date, I was kinda complicit in that one. You were definitely not going to be relieved of your virginity that night, and not by that guy."

Hadley searched his carefully blank expression, seeing what he didn't say. "You were following us, weren't you?"

He shrugged. "It was as much to keep you safe as to keep your brother out of jail."

Rolling her eyes, she stepped back. "Men. God forbid you trust *my* judgment about anything."

"It was never about not trusting your judgment. It was about not trusting the guys. Because, as you have just pointed out... *men.*"

She could hardly argue when her life had taken such a sharp left turn not long after she'd been out from under their protection.

"So, what did he say?"

"The primary takeaway from the whole conversation was that he's happy for us."

Hadley let that soak in and wasn't quite sure she believed it. "Marriage has mellowed him."

"Seems like."

"I still feel like I owe it to him to talk to him myself, since I'm the reason you sat on this for so long."

Cash looked her over in that way she knew was analyzing everything. "Are you feeling up to that?"

Her level of don't-wanna was pretty damned high. But he'd done his part. It was time to suck it up and do hers. "Putting it off isn't gonna make it any easier." She crouched to pull on her second bootie. "Was he headed home?"

"Yeah. They were expecting us for dinner in an hour, anyway. I'll come with you."

She laid her hands on his forearms, rising to her toes to brush a kiss over his lips. "No. I think I need to do this on my own. Give me a twenty- or thirty-minute lead?"

"I can do that. I have a few phone calls to return."

"Take care of business. I'll see you over there."

She made it halfway to the door before he snagged her hand. "Hadley?"

"Yeah?"

He lifted her hand and pressed a kiss to her palm, brown eyes steady on hers. "I'm glad we don't have to hide anymore."

Heart fluttering, she smiled. "Me, too."

The warm, gooey feeling in her chest stayed with her until she pulled into the driveway. Not allowing herself a moment to wallow in the anxiety lurking beneath the surface, Hadley shut her car door and looked at the house, dreading going inside just as much as she had been three days ago.

Stop being a chicken shit, Steele.

Squaring her shoulders, she headed up the walk. Because they were expecting her, she didn't knock. The quiet snick of the door was lost in the clatter of dishes and pans from the kitchen. Dinner prep was clearly underway. Following the noise, she found her brother nibbling on his wife's neck as she tried to chop some vegetables for whatever was for dinner. Maddie was ensconced at the kitchen table, surrounded by worksheets.

"You know, you really shouldn't do that while your wife is holding a knife. Fingers are important."

Cayla lifted her free hand to comb through the hair at his nape. "Much as I'm enjoying this, she's not wrong, and I need to finish chopping these carrots."

Holt shot a narrow-eyed glare in her direction, but his grin took the heat out of it. "Spoil-sport."

Maddie abandoned her homework in favor of hitting Hadley with a tackle hug. "Play with me!"

Hadley stroked her hair. "I'll play with you in a bit, okay? I think you still have some homework to do, and I need to talk to your dad." It was a weird thing to say, though Holt had absolutely claimed Maddie as his, even before the adoption went through.

"Can I have another marker tattoo?" She folded her hands in prayer position and deployed The Eyes. Hadley recognized the tactic as one she'd used to great effect at that age.

"If there's time before or after dinner."

"There will be time!"

Smiling, Hadley headed for the door to the backyard, jerking her head at her brother. He and BB trailed her outside. The air was cooling with the onset of sundown, and Hadley crossed her arms, ranging herself next to her brother as they both watched the dog sniff the perimeter of the yard.

Do it fast. Like ripping off a Band-aid. "So, Cash said he talked to you."

"Yeah."

"How upset are you, really?" Maybe he hadn't been honest about it with Cash.

"Are you happy?"

That made her look at him because it was a loaded question. He stood beside her, big arms folded across his chest, his blue eyes steady on hers. "With him?"

Holt jerked a nod.

"Yeah. We didn't expect it to be like this. I wasn't expecting this to turn into anything serious. I thought we'd satisfy our curiosity and be done. That's not what happened."

"Life often surprises us. My marriage is proof of that."

"True enough." After the last few days, she wasn't sure she could handle any more surprises.

With one hand, he tweaked the ends of her hair in an old gesture of affection. "Why didn't you want to tell me?"

"I legit thought you'd want to pound on him. You've always been so overly protective. It's why I've never told you about anybody I've dated."

"It was my job to protect you growing up, when you were too young to be able to do it yourself. I used to be a stupid teenage boy. I knew how they thought, so yeah, I was gonna look out for you. But I never would have worried about you with Cash. He's not a man who plays with anybody. He certainly wouldn't play with you. You both built this whole thing up in your heads for what I was gonna do, based on—I don't know—assumptions or conventions or something. If he'd been sniffing around when you were eighteen, that would have been a very different conversation with the age gap. But you're a grown adult now. I don't have any right to interfere in your love life unless I find out that somebody is treating you poorly. I know he won't." He draped his arm around her shoulders and squeezed. "It seems like you make each other happy, so I've got no reason not to be happy for you."

She shot him some side eye even as she leaned into his familiar comfort. "That's it? That's all you have to say about it?"

"Yeah. I know he'll treat you well. I know everything he was prepared to give up for you, if I didn't react well. It tells me he's serious. Are you?"

She thought of the life growing inside her. "It would be hard not to be at this point." Resting her head against his shoulder, she sighed. "He's pretty amazing."

"Yeah, he is. Big-picture-wise, I think you'll be good for him. He can be too serious, too buttoned down. You'll combat that just by being who you are."

It was Hadley's turn to laugh. "Yeah, I do a lot of that. He's stable. So very stable—in a good way. That's good for me, too."

"I never would've imagined you two together, but the idea's growing on me. Are you hanging out in serious see-where-it-goes territory or long-term potential?"

He really was being remarkably chill about this whole thing. She'd have laid odds on him making all kinds of assumptions and demands on how they ought to proceed from here. It was nice to be surprised and not have any more pressure on that front. It was a weighty decision either way.

She thought about the conversations she'd had with Cash since yesterday. He'd insisted he wanted her, no matter what. That he wouldn't judge her, whichever way she chose. That he'd be there with her, by her side, supporting her. She believed him. And because she did, she admitted the truth. "Yeah, I think we're thinking long term. We were already thinking about it, whether we admitted it or not, and now, it'll be what's best for the baby."

The arm around her stiffened, and he pivoted to face her. "You're pregnant?"

Faced with his complete and utter shock, all she could think was *Oops*.

Apparently, Cash hadn't told him everything after all.

9

Cash managed to wait twenty minutes before going after Hadley. He wasn't actively worried about her, but he didn't like the idea of them not being a united front, no matter how well her brother had taken the news of their involvement. He parked beside her car in the driveway and was about to head for the front door when Holt's voice rang out from somewhere behind the house.

"You're pregnant?!"

Oh, shit.

Changing directions, he raced for the fence, vaulting over the chain link, rather than trying to find the gate. B.B., sensing a game was afoot, came bolting across the yard for an interception as he barreled toward the back patio, where Hadley stood with her brother.

She spotted him first. "I didn't realize you hadn't told him that part."

Skidding to a stop beside her, he pivoted to escape the jumping dog. "Not mine to tell." If she elected to end this pregnancy, he didn't see any reason that information should go beyond the two of them. "I should have clarified before you left."

Did it mean something that she'd told Holt? Or was it simply a slip of the tongue because she'd thought he already knew? Not willing or ready to go down that rabbit hole, he ranged himself slightly in front of her, close enough to see the flat fury in his friend's gaze, despite the low light.

"Is this why?" Holt demanded.

"Why what?" she asked.

Why he wanted to marry her. Why he was in a hurry. Why he couldn't wait. Cash understood all of it and the concern that lay beneath the sudden animosity.

"No. I literally found out this morning, and as you're well aware, we've been here for days."

"Okay." Holt blew out a slow breath and scrubbed both hands over his face. "Okay." His gaze bounced from Cash to Hadley and back again, the gears in his big-brother brain clearly grinding and popping as he tried to process the information. "You two are having a baby. Holy shit."

Before he could go further down that track, Cash interjected, "It's early yet. She hasn't decided one way or the other what we're going to do about that." He had no idea where Holt fell on this issue, but he was prepared to do whatever was necessary to shield Hadley if he didn't approve of her choice.

"Actually, I have."

As her slim hand slid into his, Cash turned, hardly daring to breathe as he searched her face. But he couldn't read the answer beyond nerves.

She swallowed hard. "I want to do this."

Was he reading this right? She wanted to do this? Have the baby? Jump into the whole parenthood thing? As if understanding his lack of clarity, she pulled their joined hands to her belly, laying them over the child they'd made.

All the emotions he'd had on lockdown since this morning

threatened to riot, but Cash held them in check. Heart hammering, he tightened his hand on hers and stepped closer. "Are you sure?"

Her mouth curved, just a little. "With anybody else, I'd say no. With you? With you, it makes sense. If I'm going to do the world's scariest thing, it ought to be with the person who helps me be fearless because I know he's always there to catch me when I fall."

"Hadley." Undone, Cash buried his free hand in her hair and pressed his brow to hers. She was choosing them. Choosing him. He knew the level of trust that cost her, and it cut him off at the knees.

Dimly, he was aware of Cayla snagging her husband. "Let's just give them some time. They're having a moment."

"But—"

"C'mon."

Quiet footsteps moved away, heading back inside the house.

They stood breathing together for long moments before Hadley pulled back, uncertain eyes searching his face. "Is this... okay with you? You've been working so hard to be Switzerland, but I thought maybe this was the direction you were leaning. And, I mean, that wasn't the only reason I chose this way, but it's a contributing factor, and if I got it wrong—"

Cash pressed a finger to her lips to stem the worried babble. "You didn't get it wrong. I'm just soaking in the news. We're having a baby." The words felt strange on his tongue. Strange, but kind of wonderful. "We're having a baby!"

He let the emotion come now, a hot flood of joy that crashed past the walls he'd erected to hold everything in and protect his heart, opening him to everything. To her. Riding the wave of it, he took her mouth in a searing kiss. She rose to her toes, pressing against him, wrapping her arms around his shoulders, and he never wanted to let her go. Now he didn't have to. Because this woman—his woman—had chosen to keep the family they'd accidentally started.

Easing her back to her feet, he grinned down at her. "God, I love you."

It wasn't until her eyes went wide that he realized what had just popped out. Shit. That wasn't how he'd meant to tell her.

Desperate that she should believe him, he framed her face between his hands. "I love you. You. I've loved you for years. And I've been in love with you for months but too afraid to say it, for fear of scaring you off. It has nothing to do with your pregnancy or you deciding to keep the baby. This is not conditional. It wouldn't have changed if you'd gone the other way on this decision. I need you to know that. To believe it."

Her fingers curled gently around his wrists. "Cash?"

Afraid he was holding her too tight, he loosened his grip. "Yeah?"

"I love you, too." Her smile spread wide. "Basically since I was thirteen. I've just been waiting for you to catch up."

They beamed at each other.

Because he couldn't resist, he dropped his hand to her still flat stomach. "This is wild."

Her face twisted with a wry smile. "Yeah, well, God forbid I do things the usual way."

"I love your way. In fact, I hope it's a girl and that she's just like you."

"You are a very brave man," Holt announced.

As one, they turned to face him, finding him and Cayla tucked in the doorway, grinning.

"Is it safe to say congratulations yet?" he asked.

Tugging Hadley against his side, Cash pressed a kiss to her brow. "Yeah. I think congratulations are perfect."

Cayla clapped her hands in glee. "Good. Then I can start planning the party to celebrate!"

"I THOUGHT you were kidding about the party." Hadley eyed the patio that had been transformed with cafe lights, coordinated festive decorations, and a long table covered with more food than a small army needed.

Cayla just grinned. "I never joke about parties. Just wait until I get a chance to plan your baby shower."

"Baby shower?" she squeaked.

"Too soon?"

"Maybe a little. I'm still getting used to the idea." Though the concept of her impending parenthood was slightly less terrifying today than it was yesterday.

She'd reached a point of being cautiously happy and maybe even a little excited about it. It was way sooner than she'd have planned, but a part of her recognized that she had so many hangups around children and parenting that, had it been left to a plan, she might never have done it at all. She and Cash would do better by their kid than had been done for them. They'd stayed up late last night, really talking about everything. Not in a rigid, must-have-everything-planned-out kind of way, but approaching their future with a hopeful dreaming that was new to them both. They *wanted* a future together, and it had been kind of glorious to imagine what that might look like.

He loved her. He was in love with her, as she was with him. Being able to trust in that after all the upheaval of the past week was such a gift. She'd meant what she'd told him. He enabled her to be fearless. It wasn't like she wasn't scared to death that she'd find some way to screw this whole thing up. Nine months—less than, really—was hardly enough time to figure everything out, and there was no instruction manual. Yeah, she couldn't think too hard about that, because she'd start freaking out again. But no matter what scary thing came down the pike, Cash would be with her. He'd help her figure out how to navigate it. And whatever they couldn't tackle together, well, that was what therapy was for.

The doorbell rang, setting Banana Bread off on another barking fit as she raced for the front.

"That'll be the start of our guests."

It turned out to be all of them. Brax and Mia came in with Leno and both their kids. Rachel and Jonah were right behind, with Otis on a leash. They all fell into what felt like a well-orchestrated dance, inserting casserole dishes—more food? Really?—into the spread, and herding tiny humans and animals out into the backyard.

Uncertain what to do, Hadley stood off to one side.

Arms slid around her from behind. "You look a little shell-shocked."

She leaned back into Cash, folding her hands over his on her belly and wondering if his gesture was on purpose or unconscious. Either way, it made her feel safe and relaxed. "My sister-in-law is a whirlwind."

Rachel spotted them first. "Does this mean the cat is out of the bag?"

Cash's laugh rumbled against her back. "Holt knows that we're together."

"Thank God. I've been dying, sitting on the news."

Mia scooped up some salsa on a chip. "I didn't think they'd ever get around to telling him."

Cash stiffened. "Wait. You knew, too?"

"Oh, brother, we all knew," Jonah said.

"Or guessed," Brax added. "Except Holt. We kept thinking he'd clue in, but... eh."

Holt divided a glare among the lot of them. "I think I resent your implication."

"It was right under your nose, dude," Jonah added.

Cayla slid an arm around her husband. "I mean... it kinda was, honey. I suspected months ago."

Because Cash hadn't moved, Hadley turned to look up at him and burst out laughing at the dumbfounded expression on his face. "I thought you were supposed to be a spy."

He grimaced. "Evidently I'm rusty. Guess it's a good thing I retired from the field."

Jonah offered him a conciliatory beer. "Can't hide love, man."

"Then it's a good thing I don't have to try anymore." Cash shot Hadley a look that had her toes curling inside her booties.

There was a chorus of "awwwww."

"I think there should be a toast to the happy couple." Brax started passing out drinks from the cooler.

When he held out a long-neck bottle, Hadley angled her head. "Um..."

"No alcohol for the mama to be," Cayla informed him.

Brax went brows up. "You're... oh. *Oh!*"

"Wait, seriously?" Jonah asked.

"Did you seriously not realize that pregnancy test the other day wasn't Cayla's?" Mia asked.

"Why should we have known that?" Brax wanted to know.

Laughing, Hadley accepted a Dr. Pepper. As their friends made toasts to their happiness and impending parenthood, she cuddled up against Cash's side, sliding an arm around his waist. He pulled her closer and pressed a kiss to her brow. Being a naturally demonstrative person, she appreciated no longer having to squash her inclinations toward PDA. She wondered how scandalized Holt would be if she gave Cash's very fine butt a squeeze. Amused by the prospect, she slid her hand down from his waist, noticing a lump in his pocket. Curious, she slipped her hand inside, her fingers closing around something hard. Figuring it was another of his tech gadgets, she pulled it out.

"What's this?"

Cash spun, and Hadley instinctively dodged, childhood

memories of keep away fueling her agility to hold the thing out of his reach.

He snagged her around the waist. "No. No. Give that back."

Giggling, she turned over her hand. The sight of the black velvet ring box had her going stock still, the can of Dr. Pepper falling from her other hand. Cash froze, and no one said a word as she flipped it open. The ring inside flashed fire in the ambient light. The artist in her swooned at the delicate filigreed setting housing the central ruby and surrounding diamonds. The woman hardly dared breathe. Unable to speak, she lifted her gaze to his.

"You weren't supposed to see that yet." His brows drew together, obviously trying to gauge her reaction.

Hadley wasn't sure how to feel. She didn't believe in getting married because of a child. She'd told him that. When had he even had time to go pick one up? Tipping the box, she read the name of the jeweler embossed on the satin lining of the top and went brows up.

"This is from Nelson Coleman." They were one of the biggest jewelers in Baltimore.

"Yeah."

She met his eyes again. "You bought this before we came down here."

He didn't flinch. "Yeah. I wanted him to know I was serious, even if you weren't ready to."

All the tension bled out at the acknowledgment. He'd bought the ring before he even knew about the baby. That was all she needed to know.

"Then yes."

Cash blinked. "Sorry?"

"I'm saying yes."

His lips began to twitch. "I haven't asked yet."

Flashing a mischievous grin, she closed the box and slid it

back into his pocket. "Okay. Then you have my answer to sit on until you decide to act." With a pat, she stepped back.

Cash grabbed her hand, staying her progress. "Well, you've done it now." As he dropped down to one knee, she heard whispered voices behind them.

"Are you getting this?" Rachel muttered.

"Why doesn't he have flowers?" Maddie asked.

"Shh!" Cayla hissed.

"If you hadn't gotten all nosy, I'd have had time to figure out a speech and some romance. But you're getting what you're getting now." He took a breath. "Hadley, you've always been the brightest, boldest, biggest light of my life. You drive me crazy in the best possible way. Drive me crazy forever. Keep my life from being dull and gray. Marry me? Please."

She stroked his cheek, reveling in the feel of his beard against her palm. "You know, for a spontaneous proposal, I think that was pretty good. It definitely worked for me. The answer's still yes."

With a laugh, he pulled the ring from the box and slid it onto her left hand.

"Kiss! Kiss!" Maddie shouted.

"Don't mind if I do." Cash rose to his feet, scooping her up in one smooth motion and capturing her mouth with his.

EPILOGUE

Cash snapped awake, ears straining for the noise that had dragged him from sleep. Was it the dog? Or had Arwen finally figured out how to climb out of the crib?

A glance at the clock and the hints of sunrise out the bedroom window told him that, either way, he wasn't going back to sleep. As Hadley slept the blissful sleep of utter exhaustion, he pressed a kiss to the trio of swallows she'd had inked on her shoulder after their daughter was born and carefully eased away from her, smiling as she rolled backward, into the warm spot he'd vacated. Some things never changed, and he wouldn't have it any other way.

Snagging a T-shirt from the chair by the bed, he shut the bedroom door behind him and padded down the hall, straight to his daughter's room. He heard her before he saw her, babbling cheerfully to Axel. The retired military dog lay on his absurdly cushy bed beside the crib, ears alert, tail slowly swishing as he listened to whatever story she told. Actually, as he caught a word here or there, Cash thought maybe she was narrating her plan for escape. That big-girl bed might not be too far off.

Arwen herself stood in the crib, hands curled around the bars. Her dark curls haloed her head like Einstein, and her diaper hung somewhere around her knees, but those bright blue eyes were wide awake. "Daddy!"

His favorite two syllables hit him in the chest, as they always did. A quick one-two to the sternum.

"Good morning, Sunshine."

He scooped her up, giving her a nuzzle as he carried her over to the changing table. She kept up a running commentary while he took care of the dirty diaper. In so many ways she was Hadley's Mini Me, but in this she took after him. Unconscious to awake in a blink. Given his wife still wasn't remotely a morning person, he usually took on the start of the day to let her try to sleep. Sometimes it worked; sometimes it didn't. As Arwen got more mobile and more loud, he feared those days of Hadley sleeping in at all were numbered. But, the least they could do was offer up coffee and food.

"Ready to go make breakfast for Mama?"

"Yeah!"

Axel rose from his bed and stretched before following them down the hall to the kitchen, his tags a quiet jingle.

Cash let the dog out to do his business and consulted with his daughter. "What do you think for this morning?"

"Acimon omeal." Arwen added a decisive nod for emphasis.

Translating that to apple cinnamon oatmeal, Cash nabbed a saucepan and carried it over to the stove. At nearly three, Arwen was definitely getting into the idea of doing things herself, so he'd been experimenting with safe ways for her to actually do that. Knowing she loved this breakfast as much as her mother, he'd peeled and finely diced the apples the night before, storing them in the fridge in a container of lemon water. He figured

Arwen could scoop them out with a slotted spoon without too much trouble. Their last attempt at this, he'd allowed her to measure the oatmeal. That had gone... okay. Axel had been happy to lap up the dry oats that had ended up on the floor.

Hearing the sounds of food preparation, the German shepherd came trotting in from the backyard, taking up position close enough to snap any bits that fell or were conveniently dropped by little hands that wanted to share.

"Okay, little bit, what comes first?"

"Coffee!" she chirped.

Cash laughed. "You do know your mama." He lifted her up to counter height. "Press the button."

Arwen enthusiastically stabbed the brew button on the coffee pot he'd prepped last night.

"Good job."

Shifting her to his hip, he gathered up the rest of the ingredients for the oatmeal and carried them to the counter. "Okay, we need four scoops of oatmeal. Can you show me four?"

With a very serious face, Arwen held up four chubby fingers.

"All right!" Cash gave her a high five, then handed over the half cup measuring cup and held the carton of oats so she could dip into it. They counted the scoops off together. He noted they had a little more than the total two cups Rachel's recipe called for, but he could accommodate for that in the water.

They went through the process again for the cut apples. A fair amount of the lemon water ended up on the counter and the dog who lingered below, but the apples themselves made it into the pot. Mostly. Cash measured the salt, cinnamon, and nutmeg himself, then let Arwen dump the little bowl of spices in. He poured in the water and gave the whole thing a stir, setting the pot to come to a boil.

Hadley stumbled in about the time the coffee beeped, her

jaw cracking on a yawn. The oversized T-shirt she wore slipped off one shoulder. Her turquoise streaked hair was braided into two thick pigtails, and she shuffled across the hardwood floors in the duck slippers Arwen had picked out for her birthday earlier in the year. She'd never been more beautiful to him.

"Mama!" Arwen stretched out her chubby little arms.

"Morning, Peanut." On a sleepy smile, Hadley leaned in to grab her, and Cash stole a kiss.

"Thought you'd sleep later."

She hummed and lingered, brushing her lips against his again before dropping back to her feet. "That's much harder to do when the bean decided to tap dance on my bladder. I swear, you planted a whole soccer team in there this time."

Arwen grabbed Hadley's face between her hands, squishing her cheeks. "How bean?"

"The bean is good. How are you?" She tickled Arwen's ribs, and peals of laughter filled the kitchen. The best sound in the world.

Cash pulled them both in, laying a hand over the swell of Hadley's belly where the bean—which was probably more the size of a banana now—rested. "He's got your energy."

"If karma gives me another morning person child, I'm sending in a petition of protest. You already outnumber me." But her smile was fond as she rubbed the baby bump.

They'd decided together that they wanted to add one more to their brood, waiting until they'd settled into their new life and Hadley's business had hit a comfortable stride. She'd gotten creative and adjusted her hours so she didn't have to give up the art she loved in the name of family. They'd made it work, and they'd keep making it work when they welcomed their son.

She'd been a lot more chill with this pregnancy. They'd survived the roller coaster ride of their first relatively unscathed and been gifted with the world's easiest kid. Parenthood had come with so many changes, and while they hadn't loved every minute, it had meant so much to them both to be able to give their child everything they hadn't had growing up. All the way down to a house with a yard, a wooden fence, and a dog.

And above everything else, unconditional love.

~

CHOOSE YOUR NEXT ROMANCE

THANK you for reading *Hung Up on the Hacker!* I hope you enjoyed Cash and Hadley's story. If you were paying attention, I know you caught the hint of what's to come with Grey and Rebecca. Their story is *Caught Up with the Captain* and you won't want to miss this second chance silver fox romance!

AFTERWORD

Dear Reader,

This story is probably not quite what you've come to expect from a Kait Nolan novel. It is, in fact, quite different from what I originally had planned for these two. But with recent events, I saw an opportunity with Hadley and Cash to put a face on a problem that is too seldom discussed with any open minds in the United States. I wanted to humanize an issue that is too often boiled down with oversimplified, reductivist thinking.

The oops baby trope is popular because the fantasy it delivers is that a baby can bring you together. That you can fall in love over the trials and tribulations of bringing a new life into the world. That the guy will stand up and not only do the right thing, he'll love you both for it.

But that's a fantasy.

Not to say it can't happen, but the reality is that pregnancy and birth and raising children is hard. It's expensive. It takes a toll on even healthy relationships when it's planned and desired. If it's not? Too often, women pay the price and the guy has the luxury of walking away. In many states, men need only relinquish all parental rights to get out of even paying child support. There's so much punitive language around the entire thing—all directed at women. As if they alone are responsible for their pregnancy, when it takes two. And that doesn't even consider stable, married couples who are using birth control and get pregnant anyway. Because literally nothing is 100% effective all the time.

An unplanned pregnancy adds significant strain on a relationship, both emotionally, psychologically, and absolutely financially. It cuts in on the ability to pursue education and better paying jobs because the costs of childcare are astronomical. There are a million-and-one reasons why a woman (or man) may choose not to have a child yet (or at all). Not being financially stable and able to support one is a huge, *huge* one. And as someone from Mississippi, who spent time working community mental health in one of the most impoverished counties in the state, I had a front-row seat to the lives of these children who weren't wanted or who were born into a family situation without sufficient resources. It's grim.

Life only begins with birth—it has to be supported for all the years after that. Resentment and poverty and potential abuse are not a quality life, and too often the opponents of abortion never think about that. Abortion is a part of basic reproductive healthcare. There's this false narrative that's been perpetuated that women (because this is never said about men) want to use abortion as birth control because they just want to sleep around. There's significant social certainty (the so-called "they say") that women who have abortions regret them and struggle with a lot of psychological trauma over them. This simply is not the case for the majority. Psychological research doesn't support either of these positions. They're just patriarchal propaganda meant to perpetuate the subjugation of women. Beyond all that, I'm of the firm belief that absolutely *no one* should be making legislation about women's bodies if they haven't taken and passed a current course on basic biology, because there are far too many men, in power and not, who don't have even a basic understanding of how the female body works beyond being a penis receptacle.

So wherever you fall on this particular issue, please consider that someone among your friends, daughters, nieces, spouses, or other women in your life has been or will be impacted in a major way by this recent removal of human rights protection in the United States and understand that her life is not somehow worth less because she lost in the procreation lottery.

Mothers have heartbeats, too.

Love,

Kait

OTHER BOOKS BY KAIT NOLAN

A complete and up-to-date list of all my books can be found at https://kaitnolan.com.

～

THE MISFIT INN SERIES
SMALL TOWN FAMILY ROMANCE

- *When You Got A Good Thing* (Kennedy and Xander)
- *Til There Was You* (Misty and Denver)
- *Those Sweet Words* (Pru and Flynn)
- *Stay A Little Longer* (Athena and Logan)
- *Bring It On Home* (Maggie and Porter)

RESCUE MY HEART SERIES
SMALL TOWN MILITARY ROMANCE

- *Baby It's Cold Outside* (Ivy and Harrison)
- *What I Like About You* (Laurel and Sebastian)
- *Bad Case of Loving You* (Paisley and Ty prequel)

- *Made For Loving You* (Paisley and Ty)

MEN OF THE MISFIT INN
SMALL TOWN SOUTHERN ROMANCE

- *Let It Be Me* (Emerson and Caleb)
- *Our Kind of Love* (Abbey and Kyle)
- *Don't You Wanna Stay* (Deanna and Wyatt)
- *Until We Meet Again* (Samantha and Griffin prequel)
- *Come A Little Closer* (Samantha and Griffin)

BAD BOY BAKERS
SMALL TOWN MILITARY ROMANCE

- *Rescued By a Bad Boy* (Brax and Mia prequel)
- *Mixed Up With a Marine* (Brax and Mia)
- *Wrapped Up with a Ranger* (Holt and Cayla)
- *Stirred Up by a SEAL* (Jonah and Rachel)
- *Hung Up on the Hacker* (Cash and Hadley)
- *Caught Up with the Captain* (Grey and Rebecca)

WISHFUL ROMANCE SERIES
SMALL TOWN SOUTHERN ROMANCE

- *Once Upon A Coffee* (Avery and Dillon)
- *To Get Me To You* (Cam and Norah)
- *Know Me Well* (Liam and Riley)
- *Be Careful, It's My Heart* (Brody and Tyler)
- *Just For This Moment* (Myles and Piper)
- *Wish I Might* (Reed and Cecily)
- *Turn My World Around* (Tucker and Corinne)
- *Dance Me A Dream* (Jace and Tara)
- *See You Again* (Trey and Sandy)
- *The Christmas Fountain* (Chad and Mary Alice)

- *You Were Meant For Me* (Mitch and Tess)
- *A Lot Like Christmas* (Ryan and Hannah)
- *Dancing Away With My Heart* (Zach and Lexi)

WISHING FOR A HERO SERIES (A WISHFUL SPINOFF SERIES)
SMALL TOWN ROMANTIC SUSPENSE

- *Make You Feel My Love* (Judd and Autumn)
- *Watch Over Me* (Nash and Rowan)
- *Can't Take My Eyes Off You* (Ethan and Miranda)
- *Burn For You* (Sean and Delaney)

MEET CUTE ROMANCE
SMALL TOWN SHORT ROMANCE

- *Once Upon A Snow Day*
- *Once Upon A New Year's Eve*
- *Once Upon An Heirloom*
- *Once Upon A Coffee*
- *Once Upon A Campfire*
- *Once Upon A Rescue*

SUMMER CAMP
CONTEMPORARY ROMANCE

- *Once Upon A Campfire*
- *Second Chance Summer*

ABOUT KAIT

Kait is a Mississippi native, who often swears like a sailor, calls everyone sugar, honey, or darlin', and can wield a bless your heart like a saber or a Snuggie, depending on requirements.

You can find more information on this RITA ® Award-winning author and her books on her website http://kaitnolan.com.

Do you need more small town sass and spark? Sign up for her newsletter to hear about new releases, book deals, and exclusive content!